Enid Blyton's STORY TIME

The stories in this edition first appeared in
Five O'Clock Tales © Enid Blyton 1941
Six O'Clock Tales © Enid Blyton 1942
Seven O'Clock Tales © Enid Blyton 1943
Eight O'Clock Tales © Enid Blyton 1944
published by Methuen & Co Ltd
This edition published 2001 by Dean
an imprint of Egmont Books Limited
239 Kensington High Street, London W8 6SA
Text copyright © 1941/2/3/4 Enid Blyton Limited. All Rights Reserved.

Enid Blyton is a Registered Trademark of Enid Blyton
www.blyton.com

Colouring of the illustrations by Clair Stutton
'Other Books by Enid Blyton' © 2000 Sheila Ray,
first published by Egmont Books Limited in
Telling Tales: Gillian Baverstock remembers Enid Blyton.
Copyright © 2001 Egmont Books Limited

0 603 56033 4

10 9 8 7 6 5 4 3 2 1

A CIP Catalogue record for this title is available from the British Library

Printed and bound in the U.A.E.

Enid Blyton's

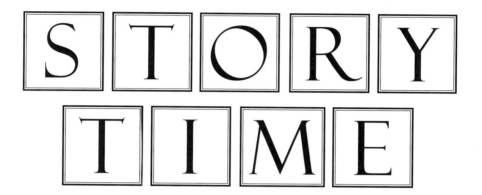

STORY TIME

DEAN

CONTENTS

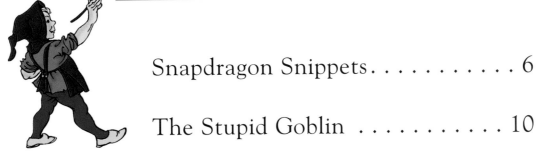

Snapdragon Snippets

The Snippet Pixies lived in the mushroom fields, where houses were cheap. As soon as a fine mushroom grew up, the Snippets snipped out a door and a window, made a stairway inside the stalk and a room inside the mushroom top, and hey, presto! there was a house big enough for two Snippets at least!

But one day it happened that a boy came along who saw the mushrooms and picked them – and, dear me, what a surprise for him when he saw the doors and windows! The Snippets flew out at once and fled away from the field. The boy followed in glee. He thought they were butterflies or moths, and as he carried a net with him he meant to catch them.

The Snippets flew on and on, panting hard. They flew over a cornfield and the boy rushed after them. They flew down the lane, they flew through a wood, and at last, quite tired out, they flew into a garden.

"We can't fly any further!" panted one little Snippet, sinking down to the ground like a tiny bubble. "That boy will catch us!"

"What's the matter?" asked a bumble bee nearby.

The Snippets told him. "There's the boy, look, coming in at the gate now!" they groaned. "Whatever can we do? There doesn't seem anywhere to hide, bumble bee."

"Quick! I'll show you a place!" buzzed the velvety bee. "Follow me!"

He flew to a red snapdragon. He alighted on the lower part and pressed it down so that the snapdragon opened its 'bunny-mouth'. In went the bee – and the mouth of the snapdragon closed behind him so that not even a leg could be seen! He pushed himself out backwards to the surprised Snippets.

"There you are! Get inside any of these snapdragon flowers and you'll be well-hidden!"

The Snippets gave little high squeals of glee. Each one flew up to a red, pink, or yellow snapdragon, and pressed hard on the lower lip of the flower. The mouth opened – the Snippets slipped in – the mouth closed up! Not a wing was to be seen, not even a tiny bare foot!

The boy banged the garden gate and looked round. "Where are those strange little butterflies?" he said, holding his net ready to catch them. "I know they flew into this garden, for I saw them. Where have they hidden themselves?"

He went to the flower-bed. He set the flowers swinging to and fro, so that he might frighten any butterfly into the air. But the Snippets were safe, though their hiding-places swung about as the boy pushed them with his net. It was like being in a cosy hammock. The flowers smelt lovely, too – they made a wonderful hiding-place!

The boy soon left the garden, and it was safe for the Snippets to come out. They peeped from their strange hiding-place and nodded to one another. "We can't go back to our mushroom houses now," they cried. "Shall we live here instead?"

Everybody thought it was a good idea. They went to buy soft yellow blankets for beds from the gnome under the hedge, and that was all they needed. Each night they crept into the bunny-mouths of the snapdragons and slept on their hammocks of yellow down, and they probably do still.

You won't find them there in the daytime, for then they are at work snipping up fallen flower petals to make frocks and coats – but you might open a snapdragon gently and see if you can find the Snippets' downy yellow beds made ready for the night!

The Stupid Goblin

One day Snip and Snap the brownies went fishing in the pond belonging to the Red Goblin. They hadn't caught more than three fish when up came the Red Goblin and pounced on them. "Aha!" he cried. "I've got you! I'll lock you up in my deep, dark cave!"

He dragged them off, and in a little while Snip began to cry loudly and say, "I've left my net behind. My nice new net!"

"Well, go back and get it quickly," said the goblin, crossly, and Snip ran off. But he didn't come back, as you can guess.

"Perhaps he has lost his way and can't find us," said Snap. "Shall I go and fetch him?" The goblin let him go – and of course Snap didn't come back either.

The next week those silly little brownies went to gather bluebells in the goblin's wood. Out he pounced and caught them again.

"Aha!" he shouted. "I've got you again. I'll lock you up safely *this* time." He dragged them off, howling and crying. Presently Snap

clapped his hand to his head and said, "I've left my cap in the woods. I shall get sunstroke, I know I shall."

"This is the sort of trick you played on me last time," growled the goblin, stopping. "I let one of you go back, and he lost his way. Then when the other went to find him, *he* didn't come back either!"

"Well, let us *both* go back for the cap together," said Snap. "Then we shan't lose our way."

"Go then, and hurry back," commanded the goblin. "I will wait here." Off went the two brownies, and though the goblin waited until midnight, you may guess that neither of them went back! No, they were safely in their beds at home!

In a few days the foolish brownies went to hunt for the first wild rose on the hedge that ran round the Red Goblin's meadows. He was waiting for them and pounced on them in delight, chuckling gleefully. "I'll lock you up *this* time!" he shouted.

But before they had gone a great distance Snip began to cry loudly and feel in his pockets one after the other as if he had lost something.

"What's the matter *now*?" asked the goblin, impatiently.

"I've left my purse full of money under the hedge," wept Snip. "Oh dear, oh dear, what shall I do?"

"Ho!" said the Red Goblin, stopping and looking slyly at Snip. "So you're trying to play me that old trick once more, are you? You want to go back for your purse and slip off home again. No, no, brownies, you can't trick an old goblin like me a third time. I shan't let *you* go again – *I* shall go and get that purse while *you* stay here!

Ha, ha, that will teach you that I'm too clever for you!"

And off he ran back to the hedge, where he hunted in vain for the purse of money. When he got back to where he had left those two brownies they were gone! Poor old goblin – he wasn't very clever, was he?

The Little Bird

There was once a little bird who told tales about other people all day long. He was a perfect little nuisance!

When he perched on Dame Winkle's windowsill one morning, he saw her putting on her shoes – and dear me, she had a big hole in her stocking. So he flew all round the town that day, whispering in people's ears, "Dame Winkle has a hole in her stocking!"

Another day he saw Snip-Snap the brownie climb over into the next-door garden and pick up some apples. The little bird flew off, and all that day he told his tale to everyone he met. "Snip-Snap took some apples that didn't belong to him!"

Nobody was safe from that little tale-teller! He peeked in at windows, he pried into every corner. Many people tried to catch him when they saw his pointed beak poking round the corner – but he was always just a bit too smart for them!

And then one day he told a tale about Goggins the witch. He

had flown down into her garden one afternoon and seen her sitting in a chair having a snooze. He had hopped nearer – and nearer – and nearer. And then he had noticed a shocking thing – Witch Goggins hadn't washed her neck! Dear, dear, dear! He flew off in delight and soon he was telling the tale all over the town. "Witch Goggins doesn't wash her neck! Fancy that! Witch Goggins doesn't wash her neck!"

Now it was a rule in that town that everyone should wash properly, and as soon as Mr Blueboy, the policeman, heard what the little bird whispered in his ear, he marched off to Goggins and scolded her sternly. The witch said she was very sorry, and asked who had told Blueboy the news.

"That little bird," said Blueboy, pointing to where the little bird was sitting on the wall, listening. Witch Goggins went indoors to wash her neck, and she vowed to herself that she would catch that little bird and punish him!

But do you suppose she could get near enough to that cunning little bird to catch him? No, she certainly could not! He flicked his wings and flew off as soon as he saw her. He wasn't going to be caught by Witch Goggins! She would probably turn him into a fly and then send a spider along to eat him!

At last Witch Goggins prepared a little can of water to throw over him, and in it she put a spell to make that horrid little bird invisible. She thought that if no one could see him, nobody would ever listen to his tales. She hid behind a curtain and waited.

And at last she got him! He flew down to peep in at the window

to see what he could spy – and the witch flung the enchanted water over him. At once he disappeared! The spell had worked.

But do you know, although he couldn't be seen he still had a voice! And he still went about perching on people's shoulders and whispering tales in their ears! He didn't dare to stay in Fairyland any longer, in case Goggins the witch really caught him the next time. So he came to our world, and he still goes on telling tales.

Sometimes people know something you would rather they *didn't* know, and when you say to them, "How did you know?" they say, "Aha! A little bird told me!" Then you know that nasty little tale-teller has been in *your* house – but you'll never see him because he is still invisible!

Lazy Kate

"Kate! Time to get up!" called Mother. Kate was fast asleep in bed. She grunted, but didn't open her eyes.

"KATE! You'll be late for school!" cried Mother.

"She always is," said John, Kate's brother, sitting down to breakfast. "She just simply *won't* get up!"

It was quite true. Kate was the laziest little girl you ever saw! Sometimes her mother ran upstairs, and pulled all the bed-clothes off Kate to make her get up – but even then she would go on sleeping, though she had no blankets on her!

"I don't know what to do with her!" said her mother, in despair. "So lazy and slow – it's really dreadful. She will never be any use to anybody!"

One morning a very strange thing happened. Mother went to call Kate as usual. No answer. She called again. Still no answer. She ran into the bedroom and shook Kate by the shoulder. Kate grunted and turned over the other way.

"Do get up, Kate!" said Mother. "It's prize-giving day at school today and you mustn't be late!"

"All right, Mother," said Kate, without opening her eyes. Her mother thought she would really get up now, so she went down to give John his breakfast. But Kate fell fast asleep again!

Then the strange thing happened. Her bed began to groan and creak, and to mutter to itself! Kate took no notice. The bed lifted up one of its feet and put it down again. It grunted loudly. Kate didn't hear.

Then the bed lifted up another foot – and this time it took a step towards the door! Goodness! What a funny thing to happen! Kate's bed was very small, and it got through the door with a squeeze. Then, very carefully, it made its way downstairs, carrying Kate with it! She was dreaming peacefully, and didn't even stir!

Right down to the bottom of the stairs walked the bed, and then, as the front door stood wide open, out it went! Nobody heard it, for the dining-room door was shut.

Down the street walked the bed, carrying Kate under the bed-clothes! How everyone stared! The children were going to school, and they ran after the bed in delight.

"Look! Look! There's a bed walking – and there is someone in it! Oh, what fun! Where is it going?"

Well, it was taking Kate to school! What do you think of that? Just as the bell stopped ringing, and all the children were standing in rows – in walked the bed at the door!

The children squealed and shouted in delight. "Look, it's come to school! Oh, do look! Who is it in bed?"

They made such a noise that Kate woke up in a fright. She sat up and rubbed her eyes – and then, how she stared – and stared – and stared. Then she went very red indeed, for she felt ashamed to have come to school in her night-dress, and in *bed*! She lay down under the bed-clothes and pulled them over her red face. Oh, dear, oh, dear!

The bed wouldn't walk home again – it liked school so much – so a van had to be fetched to take it and lazy Kate back home.

And do you suppose Kate was ever late again?

No – as soon as that bed gives so much as the smallest creak Kate is out on the floor, dressing!

Are any of you sleepyheads? Be careful your bed doesn't behave like Kate's.

You Can't Please Everybody!

Flip and Flap were two jolly gnomes who tried to please everyone. But once they tried too often, as you shall hear!

It happened one day that they wanted to go to market to fetch some potatoes in their barrow and Flap thought it would be a good idea to take with them a sack of apples to sell. So they fetched the big wheelbarrow and filled a sack full of their best apples. Then they set off.

Now Flip was very tall and thin and Flap was very short and stout, so they looked an odd pair. Flip wheeled the barrow and Flap took the sack of apples on his fat shoulder. It was a hot day and the road to the market was a long one. Many people were going to market that day, and some of them stared laughingly at the two gnomes.

"Look at that little fat one carrying the sack!" cried a big brownie, pointing his long finger at Flap. "What foolish gnomes they are! Why don't they put the sack in the barrow and wheel it? Then it need not be carried!"

"Dear me!" said Flip, stopping and looking at Flap. "We might have thought of that, Flap. Put the sack of apples in the barrow and I can easily wheel it."

So Flap thankfully put the sack into the barrow and walked on his way, glad to be rid of his load. But tall, thin Flip found the barrow rather heavy to push and every now and again he gave a little groan. Some pixies passing by heard him and they stopped and pointed their fingers at fat Flap, swinging along by himself, whistling.

"Look at that strong, fat gnome selfishly walking by himself, letting his poor thin brother push that heavy barrow!" they cried. "For shame! He ought to push the barrow himself!"

The gnomes stopped and Flap went very red. He took the handles of the barrow from Flip at once.

"Better let me push the barrow, Flip," he said. "I don't want people to think I am selfish, for I am much too fond of you to be unkind. You walk and I will take the barrow."

So tall, thin Flip walked beside the barrow whistling merrily, while short, fat Flap pushed it. The sun was very hot indeed and soon Flap panted and puffed with the heat. He pushed the barrow along, and felt little drops of water running down his face, because he was so hot.

A large gnome and his wife came jogging up on their donkey and the wife pointed her finger at Flip in disgust.

"Look, husband," she said, "do you see that tall gnome there walking by his poor little brother who is working himself to death pushing that heavy barrow? For shame! Why doesn't he help him? Surely he could give him a hand?"

Then it was Flip's turn to go red. The tall gnome stopped and looked at Flap, who was still puffing and panting as he pushed the barrow.

"Look here!" said Flip. "Hadn't we better push the barrow together, Flap? You can take one handle and I can take the other. Then everyone can see we are helping one another."

So Flap took the right handle of the barrow and Flip took the left handle, and off they went again down the road.

Very soon a big party of pixies rattled by in a wagon, and when they saw the two gnomes both pushing the one wheelbarrow they screamed with laughter and pointed their small fingers at them in scorn.

"Look! Look! Those gnomes are so weak and feeble that it needs both of them to push one barrow! Oh, what a funny sight! Poor things! They ought to eat lots of eggs and butter to get up their strength. Then it wouldn't need two of them to push one small barrow!"

The gnomes put down the barrow with a bang and stared angrily after the cheeky pixies.

"*Well!*" said Flap, snorting down his nose in rage. "We can't seem to please anybody this morning! What are we to do now?"

"Well, it's no use one of us carrying the apples and the other

wheeling the barrow," said Flap, "because we were laughed at for that."

"And it's no good you wheeling the barrow alone, or me wheeling it either," said Flap gloomily, "because people think we're selfish then."

"And they think we're poor, weak things if we wheel it together," said Flip. "But wait – *I* know what we'll do, Flap! You carry the barrow over your shoulder, and *I'll* carry the sack of apples! Then we shall neither of us be called stupid, selfish or feeble. Isn't that a good idea?"

"Fine!" said Flap, and he hoisted the barrow on to his head. The weight of it bent him over and he couldn't see where he was going, so he told Flip to walk in front of him and guide him.

Flip went in front and together they made their way to the market. The road began to get very crowded, and pigs, hens and ducks were all over the place. Suddenly a little pig ran between Flip's long legs and over he went with the bag of apples. They rolled all over the road and the pigs gobbled them up at once! Then Flap fell over Flip and down came the barrow, crash! Its wheel broke in half and both the handles were cracked.

"My goodness me!" said Flap, sitting up and looking in dismay at the pigs gobbling the apples and at his broken barrow. "Look at that, Flip! This is what comes of trying to please everybody! *Next* time we will please ourselves!"

And I really think it would be better if they did, don't you?

The Adventurous Clown

There was once a clown called Tuffy, who lived in a toy shop with hundreds of other toys. Some of them were very grand toys who wouldn't even look at the little clown, with his painted face and pointed hat. Some were not so grand and the clown would often talk with them.

Tuffy the clown longed to be a hero. He longed to do something grand, something noble so that all the toys in the toy shop would cheer him and cry out that he was a hero. He thought his little corner on a toy shelf was dull. Nothing ever happened there. How could he be a hero when nothing ever happened?

"Why do you grumble so?" asked Timothy, the puppy dog with boot-button eyes and a tail that really wagged. "Be happy and contented with us, Tuffy. We are a nice little family here on this shelf. Why do you want to go off and have adventures? They might not be nice."

"Oh, yes, they would be," said Tuffy. "Adventures are always exciting. I want to do something really fine. Save someone from a fire or something like that. That would make all the grand toys sit up and take notice. It's so dull up here on our shelf. Why, we only get dusted once a week!"

That night Tuffy the clown climbed down from his shelf. He had made up his mind to seek adventures. There must be lots of them down in the shop. He had heard all sorts of exciting noises at night. Surely grand things must happen down in the shop!

Now that night there was to be a grand race between two wooden horses and carts, driven by wooden farmers. The race was just starting as Tuffy climbed down to the floor. One cart came racing by Tuffy, the farmer standing up and yelling for all he was worth.

Tuffy stood and gaped.

"Goodness! An adventure already!" thought Tuffy. "A runaway horse! Ha, now is my chance to be a hero!"

The horse and cart came round again, and Tuffy sprang at the reins. He held on to them and dragged the horse to one side. The cart fell over with a crash, and the farmer tipped out. Tuffy stood by, helping him up, feeling very proud that he had stopped the horse.

But the farmer was terribly angry.

"What do you mean by spoiling my race like that!" he yelled. "Now the other horse and cart will win! And look at my cart, all on its side! And I've spoilt my best hat, too! You silly, interfering little clown. Take that – and that!"

And the farmer cracked his whip at poor, astonished Tuffy.

"Ooh!" cried Tuffy, rushing away. "You don't understand! I'm a hero!"

He ran out of sight, and sat down in a toy farm, wiping the tears from his eyes. Horrid man! How dare he crack his whip at him like that when Tuffy had tried to be a hero?

As Tuffy sat there he noticed a doll's house in a corner of the shop – and, dear me, what was that coming out of one of the bedroom windows, in great curls? It was smoke!

"Fire, fire!" yelled Tuffy, jumping to his feet at once. "Another adventure! Fire! I'll put it out at once!"

He rushed to get a ladder leaning against a haystack. He put it up against the wall of the doll's house. Then he found a big bucket which he filled with water from the farm pond. Up the ladder he went, yelling: "Fire, fire!"

He threw all the water in at the window, and was just going to climb down for another bucketful, when someone caught him by the collar and roared:

"And what do you think *you're* doing, playing a silly trick like that!"

Poor Tuffy was hauled in through the window and shaken like a rat. "D-d-don't d-d-do that!" he panted. "I'm a hero! I was p-p-p-putting out the f-f-f-fire!"

"Fire! What fire?" said the angry voice, and Tuffy saw that he was speaking to a sailor doll who was smoking a large pipe. "Can't I smoke my pipe without you coming and throwing water all over me? I'll teach you to throw water at people!"

The sailor doll dragged poor Tuffy downstairs and held his head under the cold water tap till he was quite soaked. Then he let him go.

Tuffy staggered out into the shop, shaking the water from his head, and squeezing out his pointed hat.

"They w-w-w-won't let me b-b-b-be a hero," he sobbed. He walked off, angry and hurt, and sat down on a seat to dry. And as he sat there he heard a cry, and looked round. There was a big globe of water nearby, and in it were swimming two fine goldfish – and in the water was a small doll!

"She's fallen in!" shouted Tuffy, jumping up at once. "I'll rescue her! This is a real adventure at last!"

He caught hold of a little net which was used to catch the goldfish when they were sold. He clambered up on to a chair and dipped the net into the water. Soon he had caught the little doll and hauled her out – but she slipped out of the net and fell bump on to the table.

She banged her head and began to cry. Up came a policeman doll and said, fiercely: "What are you doing, catching that doll and making her bump her head like that?"

"I was saving her from drowning!" said Tuffy. "I am a hero. You ought to cheer me!"

"I was having such a lovely swim!" sobbed the little doll. "I am a swimming-doll, policeman, and I swim with the goldfish every night. But that horrid clown caught me in a nasty net, and I fell out of it and bumped my head. He isn't a hero. He's just a great, big, interfering NUISANCE!"

"You'd better come along with me," said the policeman, jerking the clown up with a hard hand. "Now then – any wriggling and I'll give you a good shaking!"

"I tell you, I'm a hero and –" began the clown, struggling hard. The policeman shook him till all his teeth chattered and his hat fell off. Then off he was marched to prison.

The policeman locked him in a room in the police station and left him there. The clown sat down and put his head in his hands.

"Adventures are horrid," he groaned. "Being a hero is silly. If only I were back again on my nice, quiet shelf with Timothy Dog and the others."

Suddenly he heard a little noise outside the window of the room. "Tuffy! Tuffy!" barked a little voice. "It is I, Timothy. Here is the key to the door, coming in at the window!"

Tinkle! The key fell to the floor and the clown quickly undid the door. He and Timothy ran off together and climbed up to the shelf. Tuffy hugged the kind little dog and thanked him very much.

"*You're* the hero!" he said. "All the things I did were silly, not wonderful or noble. I didn't stop to think. But you saw I was in real trouble and saved me."

"Don't mention it," said the toy dog, blushing. "I don't want to be a hero, I'm sure."

"Oh, how lovely and peaceful it is up on this shelf," said Tuffy, looking round happily. "I never want to leave it again."

And, until he was sold, he never did!

Quizzy the Goblin

Quizzy was a small green goblin who was always poking his long nose into everything. He really was a perfect nuisance. He wanted to know this and he wanted to know that. He always longed to know every secret there was, and if people wouldn't tell him he flew into a rage and blew green flames out of his mouth.

So nobody liked him very much, and most people were afraid of him. He lived in a hole in the middle of an apple tree that tapped against a nursery window. He often ran up the tree and, if the window was open, hopped into the nursery.

Then the toys would sigh and say: "Oh bother! Here's Quizzy again. Now we shan't have any peace at all!"

Quizzy wanted to know everything. He wanted to know how to wind up the clockwork engine, and how to set the clockwork mouse going. As soon as he knew, he set the engine and mouse going, and they bumped straight into one another. The mouse hurt his nose, and the engine had a bump on its front. They were very cross.

But Quizzy laughed till the tears ran down his cheeks. That was the sort of thing he thought was really funny.

Then another time he wanted to know how the musical box worked, and he wound the handle round so often that it became worn out and broke. The toys were very angry about that, for they loved the tinkling music that came out of the musical box. The clockwork clown scolded the goblin for breaking it, and he flew into a rage at once.

Green flames shot out of his mouth and burnt a hole in the nursery carpet. The toys were frightened and rushed to the toy-cupboard. They climbed in and shut the door – but that wicked little goblin blew a green flame through the key-hole and burnt a hole in the big doll's dress. She screamed, and the goblin laughed loudly.

"That will teach you to interfere with me!" he cried. "I shall do exactly as I like in your nursery, so there!"

With that he jumped out of the window and disappeared down the apple tree. The toys were so glad to see him go.

"If only we could give him a real fright so that he would never come back again!" sighed the big doll, trying to mend the hole in her pretty blue dress.

"But we can't!" said the clockwork clown. "Because, for one thing, he would never go near anything he was afraid of – and for another thing I don't believe there *is* anything he is frightened of!"

Now the very next day what should come to the nursery but a large red box in which was hidden a jack-in-the-box with a very long spring to make him jump right out as soon as the lid was opened.

The toys all knew what a jack-in-the-box was, for there had been plenty in the toy shops where they came from – but they wondered if the goblin knew. Perhaps he didn't! If he didn't, what a fright he would get if only they could make him open the box! But how could they make him? If they told him to he would certainly think there was some trick about it, and wouldn't go near it!

"I know!" said the clockwork clown, who was always the one to get good ideas. "I know! Let's pretend to hide the box away, and beg the goblin not to touch it. Then he is sure to wonder what it is, and he is such a one for poking his nose everywhere that he is certain to lift up the lid sooner or later – then whooooosh! The jack-in-the-box will jump out, and *what* a fright he'll get!"

The big doll wrote out a notice and put it against the box. The notice said: "*Do not touch!*"

"That will make the goblin want to touch it as soon as he sees it!" said the doll, with a laugh.

The next time the goblin came in at the window the toys caught hold of the box and pretended that they were trying to hide it away from Quizzy. He saw them at once and ran up.

"What's that you're trying to hide away?" he cried. "Is it a secret?"

"Yes, it is, and *you're* not to find out our secret!" cried the teddy-bear.

"What's in the box?" shouted Quizzy, excitedly.

"Never you mind!" said the clockwork clown.

"Is it gold?" asked Quizzy. "Or something nice to eat? Or fine new clothes?"

"It doesn't matter what it is, you're not to look and see!" said all the toys together.

Well, of course, that made Quizzy more determined than ever that he *would* peep inside that box and see what there was in it. How dare the toys have a secret he didn't know.

He didn't quite like to make the toys show him the inside of the box, when they were all so determined not to, so he made up his mind to come back just before cock-crow, when the toys would have climbed into the toy-cupboard to sleep. Then he would open the box and find out the great secret! And if it was gold he would take it for himself. If it was something nice to eat, he would eat it – and if it was fine clothes he would wear them. Ha ha! That would teach the toys to keep their secrets from Quizzy the goblin!

He jumped out of the window. The toys smiled at one another. They knew quite well he would come back at cock-crow!

They were all in the toy-cupboard, peeping, when Quizzy did come back. He tiptoed across the nursery floor to where the box stood with its notice leaning against it: *"Do not touch!"*

The goblin tore the notice in half. Then he looked at the lid of the box. How was it opened? Ah! There was a little catch. If he slipped that back he could open the lid.

He pressed it back. The lid flew off with a bang, and

whoooooooosh! Out leapt the jack-in-the-box, squeaking with all his might, his red face shining, his black hair standing up on end! He knocked the goblin flat on his face, and then hung over him, wobbling about on his long spring, a really fearsome sight!

The goblin got up and gave one look at him. Then he yelled with fright and tore to the window as fast as he could run.

"A witch, a witch!" he cried, and jumped right out of the window. Down the apple tree he slid and landed bump on the ground. Then he began to run. He ran, and ran, and ran – and, so the toys say, he is *still* running! Anyway, he has never come back, and you should see the jack-in-the-box laugh when he tells the tale of how he frightened Quizzy the goblin. You'd love to watch him!

The Spotted Cow

There was once rather a vain cow. She was plain white with two nice curly horns. She thought she looked rather nice – but she did wish she could have some nice black spots over her back. There were no spotted cows in the field at all, and the white cow thought it would be grand to be the only spotted cow.

Now one day, when she was munching the long, juicy grass that grew in the hedge, she came across a small pixie mixing black paint in a pot.

"What are you doing?" asked the cow.

"I'm mixing my black paint," said the little fellow. "I'm the pixie that paints the spots on the ladybirds, you know."

"Oh!" said the cow. "Well, will you paint some on me?"

"Yes, if you'll give me a nice drink of milk," said the pixie.

"I don't mind doing that," said the cow. "You can find a tin mug, and milk some of my creamy milk into it for yourself."

"I'll just finish these ladybirds first," said the pixie, and he turned back to his work. In a long line stood about twenty ladybirds with bright red backs and no spots. The pixie neatly painted seven black spots on each red back, and the ladybirds flew off in delight.

When he had finished his work he looked at the waiting cow. "I'll go and find my mug," he said. "I'm very thirsty, and I'd love a drink of your nice milk."

He ran off and came back with a mug. On it was his name: "Pixie Pinnie". He milked the cow, and took a mugful of her creamy milk. Then he began to mix some more black paint.

"Are you sure you'd like *black* spots?" he asked. "You wouldn't like a few blue ones, or red ones? You would look most uncommon then."

The cow thought about it. "No," she said at last. "I don't think so. I'd rather have black spots. They will look smarter than coloured ones."

"Well, you must stand still," said the pixie, "or I might smudge the spots, and that would look horrid. Now then – are you ready?"

The pixie began to paint the cow. Goodness, you should have seen him! A big black spot here, and a little one there! Two by her tail, and three down her back. Four in a ring on her nose, and a whole crowd of spots down her sides. She *did* look grand!

At last the pixie had finished. He put away his paints, took another drink of milk, and said "goodbye". The cow left him and went back to the field. How grand she felt!

The other cows stared at her. They didn't know her. Who was this funny spotted cow?

"Don't you know me?" said the cow, proudly. "I've grown spots."

"Rubbish!" said the biggest cow. "Grown spots, indeed. You don't belong to us. Go away, you horrid, spotted creature, we don't want anything to do with you!"

Just then the little boy who looked after the cows came along to see if they were all right. When he saw the spotted one he stared in surprise.

"You're not one of our cows," he said. "You must have wandered in here from somewhere else. You had better get out of the field, and go back to your own meadow, wherever it is! What an ugly, spotted creature you are! I'm glad you're not one of *our* cows!"

He opened the gate and pushed the surprised cow out. She trotted down the lane angrily. "I'll go to the next field," she thought. "The cows there will be pleased to have such a fine spotted creature as I am!"

But they weren't pleased! They mooed at her and sent her away. She was very miserable.

"I wish I hadn't got spots now," she thought to herself. "It was a mistake. I'll find that pixie, and ask him to take them away."

But he was gone. She couldn't see him anywhere. Then it began to rain. The cow stood under a tree to shelter herself, but the rain was so heavy that she was soon wet from horn to tail – and, dear me, the black spots all came out in the rain! Soon there were none left at all.

The cow didn't know that the rain had washed the black spots away. She stood there, feeling lonely and miserable, and when the rain had stopped she made up her mind to go back to her own field, and ask the other cows to have her back again. So off she went, whisking her big tail from side to side.

The little boy was still there. He saw her as she came, and now that she had no spots, he knew her for one of his own cows. So he opened the gate, and let her through, saying: "Dear me, wherever have you been?"

The other cows crowded round her, for, now that she had no spots, they knew her too.

"We are glad to see you," they said. "Do you know, a horrible spotted cow came in your place, and said she was you. She's gone now, thank goodness. Ugly creature that she was! How dared she say she was you, for you are so white and pretty!"

The cow didn't say anything. She listened and hung her head. It was better to be white and pretty than to be handsome and spotted. She didn't look so grand now, but she was herself.

"I hope that pixie doesn't give me away," she thought. "The cows *will* laugh at me, if he does!"

But I don't expect he will!

The Cross Caterpillar

Once upon a time there was a little green and yellow caterpillar who lived on a big green cabbage with his brothers and sisters. He hadn't been very long hatched out of an egg but he didn't know that. He was just a bit bigger than the others, and he thought himself very grand indeed.

He ate all day long. He chose the tenderest and juiciest bit of cabbage for himself, and was very angry if another caterpillar dared to share it. He would stand up on his tail end then and look very fierce indeed.

He grew bigger and bigger. He had a few hairs on him here and there, and as he grew bigger they grew longer. He was an artful caterpillar too. He knew quite well that if a shadow came across the cabbage it might be a bird hunting for caterpillars and then he would huddle into a crinkle of the cabbage and keep as still as a stalk. Some of his brothers and sisters were eaten, but not the artful caterpillar. Oh, no, he was far too clever.

One day, when he was quite big, a pretty fluttering creature came to the cabbage. It was a white butterfly with black spots. It sat down on the cabbage and waved its feelers about. The caterpillar peered over the edge of the cabbage leaf and looked at it. When it saw that it was a mild and harmless-looking creature, the caterpillar flew into a temper and cried, "Get off my cabbage! I was just going to eat this leaf!"

"Gently, gently!" said the butterfly, looking at the cross caterpillar. "This is as much my cabbage as yours, caterpillar."

"It certainly isn't!" said the caterpillar, standing up on his hind legs and waving himself about. But the butterfly was not at all frightened. It opened and closed its lovely white wings and laughed.

"You don't know what you are talking about," said the butterfly. "I have come to lay my eggs here. I shall lay them on the underneath of the leaf you are sitting on. It is, as you have found out, a tender, juicy leaf, fit for my eggs."

The caterpillar was as angry as could be. The butterfly took no notice of it at all. She began to lay neat little rows of eggs in exactly the place where the caterpillar had planned to eat his dinner. It was too bad!

"Now don't you dare to touch my eggs!" said the butterfly, warningly, as she flew off. "If you do, I'll tell the pixie who lives by the wall, and she will come and tell you off!"

The caterpillar was so angry that he couldn't say a word. But after a while he found his voice and began to talk to the others about it.

"Brother and sister caterpillars," he said. "We cannot stand this. Why should those horrid, ugly, flapping butterflies come and steal our cabbage for their silly eggs? Why should they be allowed to laugh at us and do what they like? Is not this our cabbage? Let us eat all these eggs up."

"Oh, no!" cried the listening caterpillars. "If we do that the pixie will come along, as the butterfly said, and she might be very cross indeed."

Just as the caterpillar was opening his mouth to talk again two more white butterflies came up, and when they saw the nice, juicy cabbage they at once began to lay eggs there. The caterpillar was so angry that he rushed at them and tried to push them off. But they flapped their big wings in his face and scared him. When they had gone he sat down and thought hard.

"*I* will go to the pixie who lives by the wall!" he said. "Yes, I will. I will complain of these horrid, interfering butterflies, and I will ask the pixie to catch them all and keep them in a cage. Then they can do no more mischief to our cabbage!"

"That is a fine idea!" said all the caterpillars, stopping their eating for a moment. "Go now."

So the green caterpillar left his cabbage and crawled down the path to the pixie who lived by the wall. She was most surprised to see him.

"I have come to complain of those hateful butterflies who interfere with our cabbage," said the caterpillar.

"Which butterflies?" asked the pixie in astonishment.

"The white ones with black spots," said the caterpillar fiercely. I want you to catch them all and keep them in a cage so that they can do no more harm to our cabbage."

The pixie laughed and laughed, and the caterpillar felt crosser and crosser as he watched her.

At last she dried her eyes and said: "Well, I will promise to do what you say if you will come to me in four weeks' time and ask me again. I will certainly do what you want then."

The caterpillar went away, content. In four weeks' time all those horrid butterflies would be caught and put in a cage. Ah, that would teach them to come interfering with his cabbage! He was pleased, and proud of himself. He began to eat his cabbage again and in two days he had grown simply enormous.

Then a strange feeling came over him. He wanted to sleep. He was no longer hungry. He felt strange. Some of his brothers and sisters felt sleepy too, and one day they all fell asleep, having first hung themselves up neatly in silken hammocks. They all turned into chrysalides, and kept as still as if they were dead.

After some time they woke up. Our caterpillar awoke first, for he was strong and big. He wanted to get out of the chrysalis bed he was in, so he bit a hole and crawled out. The sun was warm and he stretched himself. He seemed bigger and lighter. How strange!

He saw a white butterfly in the air and at once all his anger came back to him. He would go to the pixie by the wall, for it must surely now be four weeks since he had seen her, and he would make her keep her promise! He set out to walk as he had done before – but to his great amazement he found himself floating in the air.

He screwed his head round and looked at himself. He was flying! Yes, he had four lovely white wings, spotted with black. He was a butterfly!

"I am lovely!" he thought in delight. "I am a beautiful creature! Look at my fine wings! Oh, how happy I am!"

He flew about in the air, enjoying the sunshine. Suddenly he heard a small voice calling to him and he saw the pixie who lived by the wall. She knew him even though he was no longer a caterpillar.

"Have you come to ask me to keep my promise?" she asked, with a little tinkling laugh. "I am quite ready to keep it! And the butterfly I will catch first and keep in a cage shall be *you*!"

The butterfly was frightened. He flew high in the air. How foolish he had been! No wonder the pixie had laughed! But how in the world was he to know that one day he would change from a green caterpillar to a white butterfly?

"I am not so wise as I thought I was," said the butterfly to himself. "I know nothing! I will be quiet and gentle in future, and I will never lose my temper again!"

Where is he now? In your garden and mine looking for a little butterfly wife to marry – and you may be sure he will say to her, "Lay your eggs on a cabbage leaf, my dear! It's the best thing to do – and don't you mind what the rude and stupid caterpillars say to you – they don't know anything at all!"

Twinkle Gets Into Mischief

Twinkle was a mischievous elf if ever there was one! You wouldn't believe the things he did – all the naughtiest things his quick little mind could think of. But one day he went too far, and tried to play tricks on Snorty the Dragon.

Twinkle wasn't afraid of anyone or anything, so when he heard that Snorty the Dragon was looking for someone brave enough to go and paint his cave walls a nice cheerful pink, he thought he would try to get the job. So off he went, carrying a fine big pot of pink paint, whistling gaily as he skipped along.

"Hello!" he said to Snorty, when he got to the cave. "I hear you want your walls painted a pleasant pink."

"Quite right," said Snorty, blowing out some blue smoke from his nostrils.

"That's a clever trick!" said Twinkle. "I wish I could blow smoke out of *my* nose!"

"Only dragons can do that!" said Snorty proudly. "And look at these!"

He suddenly shot out five enormous claws from each foot – but Twinkle didn't turn a hair.

"Splendid!" he said. "But what a business it must be for you to cut your nails, Snorty! I should think you would need a pair of shears instead of scissors!"

The dragon didn't like being laughed at. He was used to frightening people, not amusing them. So he glared at Twinkle, and blew a flame out of his mouth.

"Ho, *you* don't need matches to light the gas!" chuckled Twinkle.

"That's not funny," said Snorty sulkily. "Get on with my painting, please, and make the walls a bright pink. And no more of your cheek, mind!"

"No more of my *tongue*, you mean!" said Twinkle, who did love having the last word. He began to mix his paint and to daub the wall with the bright pink colour. The dragon walked out in a huff and left him to it.

The cave was large and it took Twinkle all the day to do even half of it. When night came there was still half left to do. So he made up his mind to do it the next day. Snorty came back, and ate a sackful of corn for his supper. He liked the pink wall very much.

"Have you heard me roar?" he asked the elf suddenly, longing to give the cheeky little creature a real fright.

"No," said Twinkle. "Do roar a bit."

So the dragon roared his loudest. Well, if you can imagine ten good thunderstorms, mixed up with a thousand dustbin-lids all crashing to the ground at once, and about five hundred dinner plates breaking at the same time, you can guess a little bit what the dragon's roaring was like. It was really immense.

"What do you think of that?" asked Snorty, when he had finished.

"Well," said Twinkle, "how do you expect me to hear you roar when you just whisper like that? I could hardly hear you!"

The dragon was so angry at this cheeky speech that he lifted Twinkle up and opened his mouth and blew smoke all over him. That made the elf angry, and he ran into a corner, very red in the face, making up his mind to play a trick on the dragon the very first chance he had!

The dragon went to bed, and soon the awful sound of his snoring filled the cave. Twinkle couldn't possibly go to sleep, so he looked round for something naughty to do – and he saw the dragon's two pet geese at the end of the cave, their heads tucked under their wings. They were fine birds, as white as snow.

"Ha!" said Twinkle at once. "I'll paint them pink. That will give old Snorty a fine shock in the morning!"

So he woke up the geese and painted the two surprised birds a brilliant pink. They looked very strange when they were finished. Then Twinkle looked round for something else to paint. He saw the dragon's cat, a great black creature, snoozing by the fire. What fun it would be to give it a pink tail and pink whiskers!

No sooner said than done! Twinkle dipped the cat's whiskers into his paint-pot and then dipped in the tail. What a dreadful sight the poor cat looked!

But that wasn't enough for Twinkle – no, he must do something even more daring than that! He would paint the dragon's beautiful brown tail! So he stole up to the snoring dragon and painted his tail a vivid pink from beginning to end. It didn't suit the dragon a bit!

Then Twinkle hid in a corner to see what the dragon would say. All the pink would easily wash off, so, after the first shock, perhaps the dragon would laugh and think Twinkle was a daring elf.

But, dear me, goodness gracious, buttons and buttercups, stars and moon! The dragon didn't think it was funny, or daring, or clever, or anything else! As soon as he woke up and saw his pink geese, his pink-tailed and pink-whiskered cat, and his own terrible pink tail, he flew into the most dreadful rage that was ever seen!

He roared so loudly that the mountain not far away had its top broken off with the shock. He blew out so much smoke that everyone for miles around wondered where the thick fog came from. He shot flames from his mouth and very nearly burned up his cave, his geese, his cat, himself and poor, frightened Twinkle!

That silly little elf was really almost scared out of his skin. Who would have thought that Snorty would make such a fuss! Goodness gracious! Snorty roared again, and blew out more smoke. Then he began to look for that naughty little Twinkle. Twinkle saw two great red eyes like engine-lamps coming towards him, and he picked up his pot of paint and fled!

How he ran! How he flew! How he jumped and bounded and skipped! And after him galloped Snorty the Dragon, smoke and flames flying behind him and terrible roars filling the air. Right through Fairyland they went, the two of them, for Twinkle didn't dare to stop for a minute.

At last the elf came to the gate of Fairyland itself, and he flew over it. The dragon came up to the gate and roared to the gate-keeper to open it for him – but the pixie shook his head.

"No dragons allowed out of Fairyland," he said.

"Very well, then, I shall sit here and wait for Twinkle to come back," roared the dragon, and down he sat, just inside the gate. And there he is still, waiting for the elf to come creeping back again.

But Twinkle is afraid to go back. So he lives in our world now, and he is really quite happy, using his paint and paintbrush all the year round. And what do you think he does? You have often seen his work, though you may not have known it. He paints the tips of the little white daisies on our lawns and in our fields! Go and look for them – you are sure to find a pretty, pink-tipped one. Then you will know that that mischievous elf, Twinkle, is *some*where near.

Call him and see if he comes!

The Enchanted Shoelace

There was once a little pixie called Skippy who went shopping in his village. As he trotted along his shoelace broke and his shoe came undone.

"Bother!" said Skippy, stopping. "Now I must buy another shoelace."

But he didn't need to buy one – for as he went merrily along he saw one lying in the road. His shoes were red, and the lace was green, but that didn't matter. It would lace up his shoe, whatever colour it was!

He slipped the lace into his shoe and tied it. That was fine. Now he was quite all right. Off he went again, skipping along, as happy as a bumble bee.

Soon he came to a sweet shop and he looked in very longingly. He hadn't any money for sweets – but how delicious those big peppermints did look, to be sure!

"I just wish I had a pocketful of those!" sighed Skippy, and on he went. In a short while he felt something heavy in his pocket, and he put in his hand to feel what it was.

Peppermints! Peppermints by the dozen!

Ooh, what a surprise! But however did they come there?

"My wish came true!" marvelled little Skippy. "Oh, what a wonderful thing!"

He didn't know that he had a magic shoelace in his shoe – a lace that had once belonged to a witch and was enchanted! It came undone and nearly tripped him up.

"Bother!" said Skippy, doing it up. But he couldn't be cross for long with a pocketful of peppermints. He saw a little white kitten playing with its tail in the sunshine. Skippy was very fond of animals and he stood and watched it.

"I do wish I had a little white kitten just like that!" he said.

"Miaow!" Something rubbed against his legs, and Skippy looked down. He saw another little white kitten, looking up at him and mewing.

"Bless me!" said Skippy, in astonishment. "If that isn't another wish come true! Well, well, well!"

He picked up the kitten and cuddled it. It nestled happily under his coat, glad to belong to a nice little pixie like Skippy. He bent down and did up his shoelace which had again come undone.

"This is really very strange," thought the pixie, tickling the kitten under the chin. "This must be my lucky day, or something. I wonder if another wish will come true."

He blinked his eyes and thought hard. "I wish my suit was made of gold!" he said.

In a flash Skippy's red suit changed to a gleaming yellow. He was dressed in gold!

"Ooh!" said Skippy, amazed. "Look at me all dressed up in gold! I'm a prince! I'm as grand as can be!"

His shoelace came undone again, and trailed on the ground. "Bother!" said Skippy. "It will trip me up as sure as eggs are eggs!"

He did it up, feeling most excited. He must tell somebody about his great good fortune. He would go to his friend Tickler the gnome and tell him. How surprised Tickler would be! Aha, he would wish all kinds of things for Tickler the gnome!

Off he went, skipping down the road as merrily as could be. What a day! What an adventure!

He banged at Tickler's door and the gnome opened it in surprise, staring at Skippy and the kitten.

"Why do you knock so hard?" he asked. "Oh, Skippy – how beautiful you look! Where did you get that fine suit made of gold?"

"Would *you* like one?" asked Skippy, beaming. "All right! I wish you had a suit like mine, Tickler!"

Hey presto! At once the gnome shone brightly in a suit as fine as Skippy's. He stared down at himself in amazement.

"Oh, Skippy!" he said. "Skippy! What's happened? Do your wishes all come true?"

"Yes," said Skippy, happily, and he stepped forward to go into Tickler's house. But his shoelace was undone again and nearly tripped him up. "Bother, bother, bother!" he said, and did it up. Then he went into Tickler's neat little house.

"I can't tell you why my wishes come true," he said to Tickler. "They just suddenly did."

"But there must be some reason why," said Tickler, puzzled. "Have you anything new on you, Skippy?"

"No, nothing," said Skippy, quite forgetting about the shoelace. "The magic just suddenly came."

"Wish something else," said Tickler. "Wish for a jolly good dinner!"

"I wish we could have a fine dinner to eat this very minute!" said Skippy at once – and lo and behold, in front of them, on Tickler's round table, appeared a most delicious dinner! A roast chicken sent its tasty smell into the air, and a meat pie stood ready to be served. A large treacle pudding appeared and a plate of big jam tarts.

"Ooh my!" said Tickler, half frightened.

"Let's eat," said Skippy. So they began to eat, and didn't they enjoy their dinner!

"I'm just going to get some water to drink," said Skippy, and he hopped off his seat to go to the tap. His shoelace had come undone again, and he fell down on the floor!

"Bother!" he said. "That shoelace is always tripping me up!"

He did it up and got his water, which he immediately wished into lemonade. Really, it was marvellous!

"Now I shall wish myself a little white pony to ride," said Skippy. "And I'll wish you one too, Tickler."

"I'd rather have a pink pony," said Tickler. "That would be most unusual."

"A pink one wouldn't be nice," said Skippy, frowning. "It would look silly. I'll get you a nice white one."

"I'd rather have a pink one," said Tickler.

"But *I* shouldn't like a pink pony," said Skippy.

"Well, it's not you who is to have it, it's me," said Tickler. "Wish me a pink one, Skippy."

"I wish for two nice white ponies," said Skippy firmly.

At once two little ponies appeared outside in the garden, as white as snow. Skippy got up to run out and nearly tripped over again. His lace was undone.

"Oh, there's that stupid lace undone again!" he cried. He did it up and went outside. "Come on, Tickler," he called, "here's your pony waiting for you. Come and have a ride."

"I wanted a pink pony," said Tickler sulkily. "I don't want a white one."

"You horrid, ungrateful thing!" cried Skippy. "Here I've got you a golden suit and a fine meal, and a lovely pony too, and all you can do is to frown at me and look sulky."

"Well, I wanted a pink pony," said Tickler. "A pink pony is uncommon. You were too selfish to let me have what I wanted."

"I'm *not* selfish!" cried Skippy, in a rage. "Aren't I sharing all my wishes with you, now? What more do you want?"

"I just want a pink pony," said Tickler, in an obstinate voice.

"Oh well, have a hundred pink ponies then!" shouted Skippy in a temper – and hey presto, the little garden was at once full to overflowing with small, bright pink ponies!

"Oh, they're treading on my flowers and on my lovely new peas!" shrieked Tickler in dismay. "Oh, take your horrid ponies away, Skippy!"

"They're not mine, they're yours!" said Skippy, dancing about in glee. "You wanted pink and you've got pink!"

He suddenly tripped headlong over his shoelace, which had come undone once more. Down he went, with his nose in the dust.

"Ha, ha, ha! ho, ho!" laughed Tickler. "That's what comes of being too proud, Skippy. Pride goes before a fall! That shoelace of yours punished you nicely!"

Skippy sat up and looked angrily at his shoe. Yes, that horrid, stupid shoelace was undone again!

"I wish to goodness I'd never put you into my shoe!" said Skippy, crossly, putting out his hand to take the lace to tie again. But it wriggled out of his fingers like a green snake and vanished down the garden path!

And at the same moment all the ponies vanished too! The little white kitten, which had been wandering happily about, suddenly shot up into the air and disappeared like a white cloud.

"Where have all the ponies gone?" said Tickler in wonder. "And oh, Skippy, where has your gold suit gone? You've got your old one on again."

"So have you!" cried Skippy. "Did you see my shoelace slide off like a snake, Tickler? Wasn't that strange?"

"Where did you get it from?" asked Tickler, suddenly.

"I picked it up in the road," said Skippy. "Ooh, Tickler! That's what brought the magic! Of course! When I wished a wish the shoelace always came undone. I remember now – and oh, oh, what a terrible pity, I've wished it away! I've wished my wonderful good luck away!"

"If we hadn't quarrelled it wouldn't have happened," said Tickler, tears coming into his eyes. "Oh, Skippy, how foolish we've been. To think we had riches, happiness, everything just for the wishing – and we quarrelled about a pink pony!"

"It shows we weren't big enough to have such a wonderful power," said Skippy. "Oh my, oh my, if ever I get a magic shoelace again, won't I just be careful with it!"

But the pity of it was that he never *did* find one again. Do be careful if *you* find one, won't you!

The Little Fat Dormouse

There was once a fat dormouse who lived in a cosy home in the hedge with his mother and father and four brothers and sisters. His name was Pitterpat because his feet went pitter-pattering like rain along the bank by his home. Pitterpat didn't like being a dormouse. He was small, too small, he thought. Why couldn't he be big, like a rabbit, or have sharp claws, like a cat? Then he would be Somebody!

He thought he was much cleverer than his family. He was always laughing at them and telling them they were stupid. At last his brothers and sisters turned him out of the nest and said:

"If you are so clever, go and find another home! Let us know when you have made your fortune and we will come and admire you – but until you have done something great, leave us to ourselves!"

Pitterpat was very angry. He picked up his little bag and set off, vowing to himself that he would soon show his brothers and sisters what a clever fellow he was. Ha, he would be a cow, or horse, or even a sharp weasel if he could find one who would teach him all the tricks.

Soon he came to a field. In it there were some sheep grazing, and Pitterpat went up to one of them.

"Madam," he said, politely. "I am a clever dormouse, but I would like to be a sheep. Will you tell me how?"

"Certainly," said the surprised sheep, looking at the tiny dormouse. "Can you baa?"

Pitterpat tried. He could squeak, but he could not seem to baa.

"Well, never mind," said the sheep. "You must grow wool on your back."

"But that would be so hot," said the dormouse. "It is summertime."

"You *must* grow wool if you want to be like us," said the sheep.

"I don't think I will be a sheep," said the dormouse and he scurried away, thinking that sheep must be stupid to wear wool in the summer. Soon he came to where a rabbit nibbled grass outside its hole.

"Sir," he said, "I am a clever dormouse, but I would like to be a rabbit. Will you tell me how?"

"Well, you must learn to make a great home of burrows under the ground," said the rabbit. "You must use your paws like this to scrape up the earth." The rabbit scraped a shower of earth up and it fell all over the dormouse.

"That's a stupid thing to do," said the dormouse, angrily. "Look how dirty you have made me."

The rabbit took no notice. "Then," he went on, "you must grow a short, fluffy white bobtail like mine. It acts as a danger-signal to everyone when I run to my hole. My friends see my bobbing tail and run too."

"My tail is much better than yours," said the dormouse scornfully. "I don't think I will be a rabbit." He ran away, thinking what a stupid creature the rabbit was, covering him with earth like that and talking about bobtails.

He came to a pond after a while and saw a fine white duck squatting beside the water, basking in the sun. He went up and bowed. "Madam!" he said. "I am a clever dormouse, but I would like to be a duck. Will you tell me how?"

"First you must quack like this," said the duck, and she opened her beak and quacked so loudly that the dormouse was half frightened. He opened his mouth and tried to quack too, but all the sound he made was a small squeal.

"And then," said the duck, "you must swim, like this!" She flopped into the water, and it splashed all over the watching dormouse, soaking him to the skin.

"You silly, stupid duck, look what you've done!" he cried in anger. "You've nearly drowned me."

"Oh, you'll have to get used to a wetting if you're going to be a duck," quacked the duck, merrily.

"I don't think I will be a duck!" called the dormouse and hurried away. "Silly creature," he thought. "Splashing me like that!"

A grunting noise made him stop. He looked under a gate and saw a large, fat pig in a sty. Ah, how big and fine he looked! The dormouse crept under the gate and spoke to the pig.

"Sir," he said, "I am a clever dormouse, but I would like to be a pig. Will you tell me how?"

"Can you grunt, like this?" said the surprised pig and grunted in such a vulgar manner that the dormouse was quite disgusted.

"I shouldn't wish to make such a rude noise as that," he said, his nose in the air. The pig grunted again and began to root about in the mud of his sty so roughly that poor Pitterpat was sent head-over-heels into a dirty puddle.

"You must learn to root about like this," said the pig, twinkling his little eyes cheekily at the dormouse. "Oh, did I upset you?"

The dormouse picked himself up out of the mud and looked angrily at the pig.

"I don't think I will be a pig," he said, huffily. "Nasty, dirty, ill-mannered creatures!"

The pig laughed gruntily, and the dormouse pattered off. Ugh! He wouldn't be a dirty old pig for anything!

Outside the farmyard he met a sharp-nosed rat. This rat was eating potato parings which he had pulled from the rubbish-heap. The dormouse watched the rat, and noticed his clever, sharp eyes and the way in which he held the food in his front paws. Ah, here was a clever fellow, to be sure! Not stupid like the rabbit and sheep, not wicked like the duck, not dirty like the pig. He would be a rat!

"Sir," said the dormouse, going nearer. "I am a clever dormouse, but I would like to be a rat. Will you tell me how?"

"Certainly," said the rat. "Can you squeal like this?" He squealed shrilly. The dormouse opened his mouth and squealed too.

"Not so bad," said the rat. "Now can you hold food in your paws as I do?" The dormouse tried, and he could do it easily. He was delighted. Ah yes, he would certainly be a rat!

"What else must I do?" he asked.

"You must learn to pounce on your victims like this," said the rat, and he leapt to one side. "See, this is how I catch a young bird! And see, this is how I pounce on a frog! And SEE! This is how I pounce on silly little dormice!"

He leapt at the astonished dormouse – but Pitterpat gave a frightened squeal and fled for his life. Down a molehole he went and into a maze of small tunnels. The rat followed him, hungry for a dinner.

The dormouse slipped aside into a tiny hole he knew of, hoping that the rat would pass before he guessed he was there. The rat did pass – and at once Pitterpat turned and fled back the way he had come, never stopping once until he had got back to his own cosy home again, high up in the hedgerow.

As he scrambled into the big, round nest all his sisters and brothers cried out in surprise. "Oh, here's the clever one back again! Have you made your fortune?"

"No," said the dormouse, hanging his head. "I haven't made a fortune but I've made a lot of mistakes. I'm not clever, I'm very stupid. Forgive me and let me live here again with you."

So his family forgave him, and the little dormouse lived happily in the hedgerow. "It's best to be what you are!" he thought. "I'm *glad* I'm a stupid little dormouse!"

The Skippetty Shoes

Mr Winkle was a shoemaker. He lived in a tiny, tumbledown cottage, and all day long he sat outside on a bench and made or mended shoes. He was a merry, mischievous fellow, always ready for a joke. Sometimes he played naughty tricks and made his friends cross.

One time he ran a glue brush inside a pair of shoes that he sold to Father Grumps – and dear me, how Grumps tugged and pulled to get those shoes from his feet! In the end both his socks came too, and Father Grumps was very angry indeed.

Another time Winkle put a squeak into the heels of some boots he sold to Dame Twisty, and when she heard the squeak-squeak-squeak as she walked, she really thought it was a goblin coming after her, and she fled down the street in fright, her shoes squeaking loudly all the time! Yes, really, Mr Winkle was a mischievous fellow.

He got worse as he grew older, instead of better. People shook their heads and said: "One day he will go too far, and then who knows what will happen to him?"

Now, one morning, as Mr Winkle sat mending shoes, and humming a little song that went "Tol-de-ray, shoes for a fay, tol-de-rome, shoes for a gnome," a fat gnome came by. He stood and watched Winkle at work, and Winkle looked up and grinned.

"You've a lot of time to waste!" he said, cheekily.

The gnome frowned. He felt in his bag and brought out a pair of old slippers, each of which had a hole in the sole. They had once been grand slippers, for there was a gold buckle on each, and the heels were made of silver.

"How long will you take to mend these?" asked the gnome.

"One hour," answered Winkle, looking at them. "My, how grand they were once – but they are very old now, and hardly worth mending."

"They are most comfortable slippers," said the gnome, "and that is why they are to be mended, Mr Winkle. Now, set to work, and keep your tongue still. It wags all day long."

"Better than growling all day long, like yours!" answered Winkle, cheekily. The gnome frowned again, and sat himself down on a stool.

Winkle tried to make him talk, but he wouldn't say a word. He just sat there and thought.

Mr Winkle felt annoyed. What an old solemn-face the gnome was! Cross old stick, thought Winkle, as he began to mend the slippers. His needle flew in and out, and his busy little brain thought about the old fat gnome.

Presently an idea came into his naughty mind. He would play a trick on the gnome. But what trick could he play? He thought and thought and then he got up and went indoors. Somewhere he had got a little Skippetty Spell – but where was it? If only he could find it, what a fine trick he would play on the old fat gnome!

He hunted here and he hunted there – and at last he found it, tucked inside a milk jug. Good! Winkle hurried back to his bench, and found the gnome looking crossly at him.

"Where have you been?" he said. "Get on with your work. I want those shoes finished at once."

Winkle made a face and sewed quickly at the shoes. Into each he sewed half of the Skippetty Spell, grinning to himself as he thought of how the gnome would kick, jump, leap and prance, as soon as he put those slippers on his feet. Ho, ho! That would be a funny sight to watch! That would teach the solemn old fellow to frown at him and talk crossly!

"The slippers are finished," said Winkle at last. He handed them to the gnome, and took his payment. But still the old fellow sat there on his stool, as if he were waiting for someone.

"What are you waiting for?" asked Winkle.

"The king is coming to call for me here," said the gnome. "He said he would fetch me in his carriage. It is his shoes you have mended. They're his oldest ones, but so comfortable that he cannot bear to get new ones."

Winkle stared in horror. Gracious goodness, were they really the

king's own slippers? He was just going to take them from the gnome when there came the sound of galloping hooves, and up came the king's carriage. The gnome stood up and went to the gate. The carriage stopped and the king leaned out.

"Did you get my shoes mended?" he asked.

"Yes, Your Majesty," said the gnome and gave them to the king. His Majesty kicked off his grand gold boots and slipped his feet contentedly into his old slippers.

"Oh, how nice to have these again!" he began – and then he stopped in dismay. Oh, those slippers! As soon as they were on the king's feet the Skippetty Spell began to work, and what a shock they gave His Majesty!

They jumped him out of the carriage. They made him kick his legs up into the air. His crown fell off into a lavender bush, and his cloak was shaken all crooked. He pranced round the garden, he kicked high, he kicked low, he jumped over the wall, and he spun round and round till he was quite giddy. Certainly that Skippetty Spell was very powerful indeed!

The gnome stared at the king in horror. Mr Winkle turned pale and trembled. When the gnome saw Winkle's face he knew that he must have played a trick. He was full of rage and he caught the trembling cobbler by the collar.

"What have you done to the king's slippers, you wicked creature?" he shouted.

"There's a Sk-Skippetty Sp-Spell in them," stammered Winkle. "Do you know how to get it out? I don't!"

Luckily the old gnome was a clever fellow, and he knew how to deal with a Skippetty Spell. He clapped his hands seven times, called out a strange magic word, and hey presto the spell flew out of the slippers, they stopped dancing, and the king sat down to get his breath.

Mr Winkle knelt down and begged the king's pardon – but he was far too angry to listen.

"Take your tools and go away from Fairyland!" roared the king. "I've a good mind to turn you into an earwig, you mischievous little creature! Go away before I think of the right word!"

Winkle was in a terrible fright. He was so afraid of turning into an earwig that he caught up his bag of tools then and there and fled right away. He ran until he came to the borders of Fairyland, and not till then did he feel safe. He kept looking at himself, to see if he were Winkle, or an earwig.

Now he lives in our world. He still makes shoes for the pixies – very tiny ones, gold and black. He has no shop now, so he has to store them somewhere else – and do you know where he puts them? I'll tell you.

Find a white dead-nettle blossom and lift up the flower so that you can peep inside the top lip. What do you see there? Yes – two pairs of tiny pixie slippers, hung up safely by Mr Winkle the cobbler!

Aren't they sweet? Don't forget to go and look for them, will you?

Inside the Doll's House

There was once a small pixie who had a large family of children. They lived in a foxglove, and each child had a flower for itself. But when the flowers fell off the foxglove there was nowhere for the children to sleep!

So the pixie moved to a rose bush. This was prickly, but there were plenty of roses there, opening in the sunshine. Each small pixie took a flower for himself, and for a few days the little family was happy. Then someone came along with sharp scissors, snipped off the roses and put them into a basket. The pixie children tumbled out quickly, and ran to their mother. She was in despair.

"It's dreadful to have so many children!" she said. "There doesn't seem anywhere that we can live in comfort. I wish I could get a proper little house, but that's quite impossible."

"There's a dear little house in that big house over there!" said a passing rabbit. "I once saw the little girl who lives there carrying this tiny house out into the garden to play with. It's called a doll's house. It would be quite big enough for you and your family, I should think. Why don't you go there?"

The pixie mother was delighted. She went with her children to the big house one night and climbed in at the nursery window. There was a fire in the room and she could quite well see everything. She looked round – and there, in the corner, stood the doll's house! The pixie gave a squeal of delight and ran to it. She opened the front door and went inside.

It was a lovely house. There were six rooms, and a little stair ran up to the bedrooms. The kitchen had a proper stove, and a dresser with plates, cups and saucers. The dining room and drawing room were full of proper furniture, just the right size for the pixies, and the bedrooms had plenty of small white beds.

"Children! Come and see!" cried the mother pixie. The little pixies ran into the house and shouted with joy to see everything.

"Now just get undressed and pop into bed," said the mother pixie, happily. "For once we will have a really good night!"

Just as the small pixies were undressing there came a loud knock at the front door. The pixie went to see who was there – and to her surprise, there stood outside a sailor doll, a teddy bear and a golden-haired doll.

"Good evening," they said, quite politely. "We have come to see what you are doing in this house. It belongs to Mary Ann, the little girl whose nursery this is. She would be very upset if her nice house was spoilt. We think you had better come out and go away."

The mother pixie sat down on the front doorstep and cried into her clean white apron. It was too bad to have to turn out just when she had found a house that suited them all so well.

The toys didn't like to see her crying. They felt most uncomfortable. She really seemed a dear little pixie.

"Please don't cry," said the sailor doll.

"I can't help it," sobbed the pixie. "All my tired little pixie children are getting undressed and jumping into those nice little white beds, and I was just making them a chocolate pudding to eat for their suppers. Can't you smell it cooking on the stove?"

The toys could. It *did* smell delicious!

"You shall taste a little," said the pixie, and she ran to the kitchen. She ladled some of the chocolate pudding into a dish and took it to the toys. They each tasted some and really, it was the nicest pudding they had ever had!

"If you'll let us stay in this house I'll often cook you things," said the pixie, looking at them with her bright eyes. "I'll make you cakes when you have birthdays. I'll sew on any buttons, whiskers or eyes that come loose. I'll keep this house spotless and tidy so that Mary Ann will never guess there's a pixie family living here. In the daytime I'll take all my children into the garden, so that no one will see them."

"Well – " said the toys, liking the little pixie very much indeed. "Well – perhaps it would be all right. Stay a week and we'll see!"

So the pixies stayed a week – and you should have seen that doll's house at the end of it. It was spotlessly clean, for all the children

scrubbed the floors, swept and dusted very well. All the saucepans and kettles shone like new. The beds were always neatly made after the children had slept in them, and the pixie had even mended a tiny hole in one of the tablecloths – a hole that had been there ever since Christmas!

Each night she cooked something for the toys – and she was a very good cook indeed. Sometimes it was a pudding. Sometimes it was a few buns. Once it was a birthday cake for the brown teddy bear. She knew how to manage the toy stove very well, and it cooked beautifully for her.

"Pixie, we'd like you to stay here," said the sailor doll, at the end of the week. "We are very fond of you and your children, and you certainly keep the doll's house even better than Mary Ann does. Stay with us, and let your children come and play in the nursery at night-time, when we toys come alive and have games too."

So, very gladly, the pixies stayed on in the doll's house – and they are still there! At night the pixie children go for rides in the clockwork train, and ride on the big elephant. They run races with the clockwork mouse and squeal like mice for happiness!

As for the doll's house it is just as spotless as ever, and Mary Ann's mother often says to her: "Well, really, Mary Ann dear, you *do* keep that house of yours beautifully! I really am proud of you!"

Mary Ann is quite puzzled – for she knows she doesn't do very much to her house. Nobody has told her that a family of pixies live there, for the toys are afraid that if she knew she might be angry.

But she wouldn't. She would be just as pleased as you would be, I'm sure!

So if you should happen to know a little girl called Mary Ann, who has a beautiful doll's house, just tell her who lives in it, will you?

Won't she get a surprise!

Mr Stupid and Too-Smart

One day Too-Smart and his friend Tiny the gnome were walking down the road together. Over Tiny's shoulder was an empty sack which should have been full of potatoes – but Too-Smart and Tiny had earned no money that day, so they had not been able to buy the potatoes they wanted.

Now just as they came up to a field-gate who should they see coming out of the field but Mr Stupid, the brownie farmer, carrying over his shoulder a big sack full of something heavy. Too-Smart took a look into the field. It was a potato field. Mr Stupid must have been digging up a sack of potatoes to take home.

"Look!" said Too-Smart, nudging Tiny. "See that sack of potatoes on old Stupid's back? I've got a plan to get them all from him! Ho ho! All you've got to do is walk behind a little way and pick up what falls out of the sack. See? *I'll* manage the rest!"

Up he went to Mr Stupid and bade him good-day. Stupid was

going very slowly indeed for the sack was too heavy, and bent him double.

"That's a heavy load you've got!" said Too-Smart, brightly. "If you promise to give me a basket of carrots, Mr Stupid, I'll wish a wish for you so that your load becomes lighter every step you take!"

Mr Stupid mopped his forehead with his big red handkerchief. The sack was terribly heavy. He looked sideways at Too-Smart and grinned. "All right," he said. "You lighten my load for me and maybe I'll give you a basket of carrots."

"I'll just tap your sack then as I wish," said Too-Smart. He waited until Mr Stupid came to a grassy path that led up the hillside to his house, for he did not want the old farmer to hear the potatoes dropping out on the road. Then he pretended to tap the sack smartly, but what he really did was to cut a hole at the bottom of it with his knife.

"I wish your load may become lighter and lighter!" he said. "There you are, Mr Stupid. Now you'll soon find that my wish will work for you."

The two went on up the hill together, and Too-Smart talked hard all the time to hide the soft plop-plop as something fell out of the sack at every step. Behind them stepped Tiny, with *his* sack – but to his great astonishment he found that it was not potatoes that fell from Mr Stupid's sack – it was stones! He couldn't think what to do – he couldn't possibly tell Too-Smart, for then Stupid would hear.

"Well, I'd better pick up the stones and put them in my sack, I suppose," thought Tiny. "Then I can show them to Too-Smart if he doesn't believe me when I say that no potatoes fell from Stupid's sack."

So the small gnome picked up every stone that fell from Mr Stupid's sack, and put them into his own. Goodness, how heavy they were!

"Well, Mr Stupid, is your load feeling any lighter?" asked Too-Smart, as he walked up the hill beside Mr Stupid.

"Oh, *much* lighter!" said Mr Stupid. "Dear me, it's wonderful, Too-Smart. I am very glad I met you, really."

"So am I," said Too-Smart. "I do like doing anyone a good turn. I told you your load would get lighter, and I've kept my word. I'm a smart chap, Mr Stupid."

"There's no doubt about it," said the old farmer, grinning to himself as he heard the soft plop of one stone after another tumbling out of his sack. He knew quite well that there must be someone behind picking them all up. Well, well, if Too-Smart thought his sack had potatoes in it, that was his own look-out! Ho ho!

Poor little Tiny panted behind them, picking up more and more stones. His sack became very heavy indeed and he could hardly carry it, for he was not very big. As for Mr Stupid's sack, it was soon as light as a feather!

When at last he and Too-Smart arrived at his house, Mr Stupid put down his sack without looking at it. He turned to Too-Smart with a smile.

"Well, you certainly kept your word," he said. "My load is much lighter now. I hardly felt it, coming up the hill. Wait here a moment and I'll get you your reward – a basket of carrots."

He went indoors, and no sooner had he gone than Too-Smart ran eagerly to Tiny, who was standing gloomily by the gate with his enormous sack of stones.

"What did I tell you?" he whispered. "Am I not a smart chap, Tiny?"

"Not so very," said the little gnome sulkily. "I suppose you know that that was a sack of *stones*, not potatoes, that old Stupid was carrying? If you don't believe me, look inside my sack. I've picked them all up and carried them. My goodness, my back is nearly broken!"

Too-Smart stared at the stones in horror. Stones! Not potatoes! Whoever would have thought of that?

Just then Mr Stupid came out with a basket of very old, very hard carrots. He walked up to Too-Smart and Tiny.

"Well?" he said to Tiny. "Did you pick up all my stones and carry them home for me? It really was very kind of you, and *such* a good idea of Too-Smart's! I can't imagine how you thought of it, but I am most grateful. My wife asked me to bring home a sack of flints to edge her new flower garden, and I can tell you it was a terrible load to carry. I was *so* pleased when kind Too-Smart offered to lighten the load for me! Thank you very much indeed!"

"B-b-b-b-b-ut . . ." began Tiny, in anger and surprise, furious to think he had carried the stones all the way home instead of the farmer. "B-b-but I thought . . ."

"I don't care what you thought," said Mr Stupid, kindly. "It was really very nice of you both. Here is your reward, Too-Smart – a basket of carrots."

He held out the basket, and Too-Smart saw what nasty old ones they were.

"You ought to be ashamed to give us those horrid carrots!" said Too-Smart angrily.

"Oh, donkeys don't mind if carrots are old or new," said Mr Stupid, cheerfully. "I don't expect either of *you* will notice the difference, Too-Smart!"

Mr Stupid picked up Tiny's sack of stones, emptied them out by the side of his wife's flower garden, and gave him back the sack with a grin.

"Goodbye," he said to the angry gnomes. "Stupid may be my name – but it isn't my nature, you know! *Goodbye!*"

He went indoors, chuckling, and soon Too-Smart and Tiny heard him and his wife roaring with laughter – and they knew why. They went home down the hill in silence, and for a long time after that Too-Smart didn't try any tricks at all.

But I've no doubt he will soon again – don't you think so?

When the Stars Fell Down

On Guy Fawkes' night little Tweeky the pixie was sitting by a puddle in the lane, eating a late supper of honey and cobweb-bread. He didn't know it was Guy Fawkes' night. He didn't know anything about fireworks at all.

So when he heard a rocket go up he nearly jumped out of his skin, and he dropped a large piece of cobweb-bread into the puddle. He was most upset.

He looked up into the sky. To his enormous surprise he saw a crowd of coloured stars dropping out of the black sky towards him. They were the stars out of the rocket, but he didn't know it. He thought they were real stars falling out of the sky, and he was frightened.

He dived under a bush and stayed there for two minutes, shivering. Then he crawled out. Where had those stars fallen? They must be somewhere about.

He began to look. He hunted over the grass at the lane-side. He searched among the stones in the road. He climbed up the bare hedge and looked along the top. No stars anywhere. Wherever could they be?

Then he thought of looking in the puddle. So he ran to it and looked into the water. Reflected there were the real stars that were shining high up in the sky. But Tweeky at once thought that they were the coloured stars he had seen falling down.

"They've dropped into this puddle!" he shouted in excitement. "They've fallen splash into this water! Now I will get them out, thread them on a string and give them to the fairy queen for a birthday present. Oh, what a marvellous thing! They have all dropped into the puddle!"

He ran off and presently came back with a net. He put it into the puddle and tried to catch the stars. He seemed to get them easily in his net, but as soon as he took the net out, alas! there were no stars there at all. It was most annoying.

Soon Grass-Green the goblin came by, and looked astonished to see Tweeky fishing in the pool.

"What do you fish for?" he asked.

"Stars!" said Tweeky, proudly. "They fell from the sky into this puddle as I was eating my supper. Red, green and blue they were – the most beautiful stars I have ever seen."

"What a surprising thing!" said Grass-Green, peering into the puddle. It was all stirred up with Tweeky's fishing, and he couldn't see anything at all. But he wanted those stars very badly indeed.

So he knelt down by the puddle and began to feel in the water with his hands.

"You're not to take my stars!" shouted Tweeky in a rage. "You're a robber, Grass-Green! Leave my stars alone!"

Pinkity the elf heard Tweeky shouting and came to see what the matter was.

"Tell Grass-Green to go away!" cried Tweeky. "He is trying to steal my stars. A whole lot fell into this puddle while I was eating my supper. They are mine! I want to thread them on a string and give them to the queen for her birthday."

"Nonsense!" said Pinkity, at once. "The puddle isn't yours, Tweeky. If Grass-Green wants to fish in it, of course he can do so! I shall fish too, and if I find the stars, they shall be mine! Make room, Grass-Green!"

Grass-Green wouldn't make room, and soon there was such a shouting and a squabbling that it woke up Old Man Pinny-Penny, who was asleep under the hedge not far off. He was half a gnome and half a goblin, and he had a fearful temper. He sat up and scowled.

"Who's making all that noise?" he grunted. "I'll teach them to scream and squabble at night. I'll knock their heads together! I'll – I'll – I'll . . ."

Dear me, the things Old Man Pinny-Penny was going to do would fill a book and a half! He got up, and went to the puddle round which Tweeky, Grass-Green and Pinkity were all pushing and squabbling.

"WHAT'S all this?" shouted Pinny-Penny, in his very biggest voice. "How DARE you wake me up?"

"Ooh!" cried Tweeky in fright. "We didn't mean to disturb you, Pinny-Penny. We will be quiet. But oh, it is so annoying of Grass-Green and Pinkity, because they are trying to steal my stars."

"Steal your stars?" cried Old Man Pinny-Penny. "Now what in the wide world do you mean, Tweeky?"

"Well, a whole lot of beautiful coloured stars fell out of the sky while I was eating my supper by the puddle," said Tweeky, "and when I looked I saw they had fallen into the puddle. So I went to get a net to fish them out. Then I shall thread them and make them into a necklace for the queen."

Grass-Green scooped through the puddle with his big hands, and Tweeky pushed him away. He hit back at the pixie, and struck Pinkity instead, splashing him from head to foot. Pinkity danced with rage and hit out with both his fists – but oh, my goodness me, he hit Old Man Pinny-Penny by mistake, and didn't that make him angry!

With a shout of rage he picked up Pinkity and sat him down in the very middle of the pool! He pushed Grass-Green who fell on his face in the puddle, and as for Tweeky, he found himself rolling over and over in the water, his mouth full of mud!

How they howled! How they roared! They picked themselves up out of the puddle and shook the water from them like dogs. Then, still howling, and shivering from head to foot, they ran off to get dry, leaving Old Man Pinny-Penny alone by the big puddle. He looked into it as soon as it had become smooth and quiet, and sure enough, he saw the stars reflected there.

"Goodness!" said Old Man Pinny-Penny, in astonishment. "So Tweeky spoke the truth. There *are* stars there after all! I'll go and get my net."

Off he went – but before he came back a grey donkey wandered down that way and saw the puddle shining. He was thirsty so he went to it and drank. He drank and drank and drank and by the time he had finished there was no puddle at all! It had all gone down his throat, stars and all!

When Old Man Pinny-Penny came back he couldn't find the puddle, though he looked up and down the lane from end to end.

"The stars have flown back to the sky and taken the puddle with them," he thought mournfully. "What a pity!"

The grey donkey watched him looking for the puddle, and he thought it was very funny to see Pinny-Penny looking for a puddle that was down his throat. So he threw back his head and laughed loudly.

"Hee-haw! Hee-hee-haw!"

But Old Man Pinny-Penny didn't know what the joke was!

The Magic Wash-tub

Binny and Tucker were doing their spring cleaning. They had moved all the furniture and scrubbed behind it. They had washed all the chair-covers and banged every book to get the dust out of them. The two pixies had worked very hard indeed, and they were tired.

"Oh dear, we've got to wash all our curtains this afternoon," groaned Binny, tying her apron strings more tightly round her.

Tucker sighed. He really didn't want to begin washing. If only washing would do itself!

That gave Tucker an idea. "Binny," he said, "do you suppose Dame Sooky would lend us her magic wash-tub for a little while? It would do all our washing for us in about ten minutes!"

"Let's go and ask her!" said Binny. So off the two pixies went. They soon came to Dame Sooky's cottage and rang her bell. Jing-jang, Jing-jang!

Nobody came.

"Bother!" said Binny. "She must be out!"

They went round the back to see if she was in the garden. No, Dame Sooky was not there – but, dear me, something else was! The magic wash-tub was there, on its wooden stand! The magic soap was inside and the scrubbing-brush too.

"Ooh!" said Tucker. "Look at that! It seems just ready for us to take!"

"Well, let's borrow it, then," said Binny. "I'm sure Dame Sooky wouldn't mind! She's a great friend of ours."

So together they carried the wash-tub home, and stood it in the garden. Then they filled it with hot water and put into it all their dirty curtains.

They stood and watched to see what would happen. In a moment or two the soap jumped up from the bottom of the tub and began to soap the curtains thoroughly. The scrubbing-brush scrubbed the dirt out of them, and then the water soused them up and down just as well as if Binny were doing it herself.

"Isn't it marvellous!" said Binny. "What a lot of trouble it is saving us! Do you think the curtains are washed enough now, Tucker? Shall we empty out the water and put some fresh in for rinsing?"

"Yes," said Tucker, and he ran to get the water. Binny emptied out the soapy water, and then Tucker poured in clean water for the tub to rinse the curtains thoroughly.

The tub soused the curtains well. Binny took them out, squeezed them dry and went to hang them up. But just as she had reached the line she heard a cry from Tucker.

"Binny! Look at our mats!"

Binny turned to look – and she saw a strange sight! All her mats and rugs were flapping along in a row to the wash-tub, which was rocking on its stand, and making a most curious noise. The mats flopped in the water and the soap and brush at once began to wash them thoroughly.

Then Binny and Tucker saw something else! They saw all their dresses and suits come marching out of the house in a line, all by themselves! They went to the wash-tub and put themselves in.

"My best dress!" shrieked Binny.

"My best suit!" shouted Tucker, and they ran to the wash-tub to pull out their precious clothes, which were already being well-mixed up with the dirty, dusty rugs and mats!

And then, how they never quite knew, both Binny and Tucker suddenly found themselves pulled into the big wash-tub too! There they were in the hot, soapy water, all mixed up with mats, rugs, suits and dresses!

The soap soaped them well. The scrubbing brush went up and down poor Binny's arms and nearly scraped the soft skin off them. Tucker was soused under the water and got soap into both his eyes. He opened his mouth to yell and the soapy water ran in.

"Ooh! Ouch!" he spluttered, trying his best to get out of the wash-tub.

Binny's feet were then scrubbed so hard that her shoes came off.

She sat down suddenly in the water and the tub nearly went over.

"Oh, oh!" she shrieked. "Tucker, save me! Oh, I'm drowning! Oh, whatever shall I do?"

The tub soused her up and down well. Then Tucker was soused and rinsed, and he gurgled and gasped, trying to catch hold of the sides of the tub to throw himself out.

Just at that moment an astonished voice cried loudly: "Binny, Tucker! Whatever are you doing?"

It was old Dame Sooky's voice. She had come in to call on Binny and Tucker on her way home – and she was most amazed to see them jumping up and down in their wash-tub, soaked and soapy. She had no idea at all that it was *her* wash-tub they had borrowed.

"Dame Sooky! D-d-d-dame S-s-s-sooky!" yelled Tucker. "Help, help!"

Dame Sooky ran across the grass – and at once she saw that it was her wash-tub, and she guessed what had happened.

And then – oh dear – Dame Sooky couldn't help beginning to laugh. She just simply couldn't! It was really too funny to see poor Tucker and Binny being washed and scrubbed in the wash-tub with so many other clothes. She tried her hardest to say the words to stop the tub – but she kept beginning to laugh again.

"Wash-tub, st-st-st-!" she began, and then she laughed again till the tears came into her eyes. "Wash-tub, st-st-stop your w-w-w-w-washing!" chuckled Dame Sooky – and oh, what a relief, to be sure! It stopped washing poor Binny and Tucker and they were able to climb out of the tub. How peculiar they looked!

"Oh my, oh my, you'll be the death of me!" laughed Dame Sooky, holding her sides.

"Well, your wash-tub was nearly the death of *us*!" said Tucker, wringing the water out of his coat. "We'd never have borrowed it if we'd known it would behave like that."

"You should have waited till I got home, and then I could have told you the words to say to stop it," said Dame Sooky. "I never mind lending my wash-tub to my friends, as you know, but not many are so foolish as to take it without knowing the right words to stop it when they want to!"

She took the wash-tub, emptied it, set it on her shoulder and went home with it, laughing so much that a crowd of little elves followed her in astonishment.

As for poor Binny and Tucker they were so tired with their buffeting, soaping and sousing that they took off all their wet things, dried themselves quickly and got straight into bed.

"It would have been easier and quicker to do all the washing ourselves in our own little wash-tub," said Binny.

"Much easier!" said Tucker. "We won't be so foolish another time!"

And then, in two twinks, they were fast asleep – and I'm not surprised, are you?

The Lonely Rabbit

Benny was a toy rabbit. He was nearly as large as a real rabbit, and he was dressed in pink striped trousers, a blue spotted coat, a bright orange scarf, and tight blue shoes. So he looked very smart indeed.

But Benny was a lonely rabbit. He belonged to Lucy, and she *would* keep leaving him about everywhere. She left him in the greenhouse one night, all by himself. The next night she left him in the summer-house and spiders walked all over his whiskers and made a web on his pretty blue shoes.

"This is horrid," said Benny to himself. "Lucy will keep leaving me alone in these nasty dark places. Why doesn't she remember to take me indoors to the nursery at night, when she goes to bed? She might know that I would like to talk to the other toys. It's a lonely life to be left by myself all day and all night."

Once or twice Lucy did remember to take Benny indoors and

then he was happy. But usually she left him on a garden seat or on the swing, when she went indoors to bed, and then poor Benny was lonely and frightened.

One night Lucy took Benny out into the field just outside her garden. She sat him down beside her and then began to read a book. In a little while some big drops of rain began to fall and Lucy looked up at the sky.

"Goodness!" she said, getting up in a hurry. "There's a storm coming! Just look at those big black clouds!"

She ran to the garden-gate, opened it and rushed up the garden path. Poor Benny was left sitting in the field!

The rain fell faster and faster. The sky darkened and night came quickly. Benny's coat was soaked through and his pink striped trousers began to run, so that a pink patch showed on the grass around him. His tight blue shoes shrank and burst right off his feet.

"This is dreadful!" said Benny. "I shall catch a dreadful cold. A-tish-oo! A-tish-oo!"

The rain pelted down and Benny sneezed again. "A-TISH-OO!"

There was a rabbit-hole just behind Benny. A sandy rabbit suddenly poked the tip of his nose out and said: "Who's that sneezing? Do come inside out of the rain."

Benny turned and saw the rabbit. He got to his feet and went to the hole. "Thank you very much," he said. "Do you live here?"

"Of course," said the rabbit, backing down the hole to make room for Benny. "This is my home. I say! How wet you are! You *will* catch cold!"

Benny walked down the hole. He was wet and shivering, and he certainly didn't feel very well. The rabbit took him to a cosy room lined with moss and dry leaves.

Another rabbit was there, and she looked at Benny in surprise.

"What are you?" she asked.

"A toy rabbit," said Benny, and sneezed again.

"Goodness, what a cold you've got!" said the second rabbit. "I think I'd better get Pixie Lightfoot here. She can look after you till your cold is better."

The first rabbit went to fetch the pixie. She came running in, a merry-eyed creature, with dancing skippitty feet.

"A-tish-oo!" said Benny.

"Goodness, what a dreadful cold!" said Lightfoot. "Bed's the only place for you. Come with me!"

He followed her down a dark passage and at last came to a cosy room in which were chairs, a table and two small beds.

"Now, undress quickly, and get into bed," said Lightfoot. "I'm going to put the kettle on the fire and make you a hot drink."

Benny took off his dripping pink trousers, his blue coat, and his orange scarf. Then he got into the cosy bed and waited for his hot drink. Oh, it was good! It warmed him all over.

"Now lie down and go to sleep," said Lightfoot. "Good night!"

"Good – a-tish-oo – night!" said Benny – and in two minutes he was fast asleep.

He was much better in the morning but Lightfoot wouldn't let him get up. No, he must stay in bed until his cold and sore throat were better. She had dried his scarf for him and she tied it round his throat. "That will keep your throat warm," she said. "Now here is some warm milk for you."

It was lovely to be looked after like that. Benny did enjoy it. It was quite different from being left about by Lucy, who didn't care about him at all. He had plenty of visitors. Both the rabbits came that he had seen the night before, and all their pretty little children. A mole came too and told him a great many stories. Everything was lovely.

Three days later Lightfoot said he could get up. "It's a fine sunny day," she said. "You can go out of the burrow and sit in the sunshine for half an hour."

"But suppose Lucy comes to look for me," said Benny, in alarm. He didn't at all want to go back to her.

"Well, you silly, just pop down the hole again like the other rabbits do," said Lightfoot. "You needn't put on your coat and trousers – they have shrunk and are far too small for you – but you must keep on your orange scarf because of your throat."

So out into the sunshine Benny went, and it was so lovely and warm there that he fell fast asleep. And while he was asleep Lucy came and found him. She lifted him up and looked at him.

"Well!" she said. "I wonder if this can be Benny. I left him here – but where are his shoes – and his pretty trousers and lovely blue coat? It can't be Benny – but this is his scarf round his neck, that's certain! Except for that he looks very like a real rabbit!"

Just then Benny woke up. He opened his eyes and looked at Lucy.

What a shock he got! He struggled and leapt down to the ground. Lucy pounced after him – but he was down the hole in a twinkling, and Lucy couldn't catch him.

"It can't have been Benny!" she thought. "It must have been a rabbit that had stolen Benny's scarf – and to think I nearly took him home. Oh, I do wish I could find Benny. I'd never leave him about again if only I could find him."

But she never did find him – for Lightfoot told Benny he could live with the other rabbits if he liked, and do just as they did. "It only needs a little magic rubbed into your fur to make you just like them," she said. "I'll do it, if you like."

So she did – and Benny became a real live rabbit like all the rest, as happy as the day was long, with plenty of company and lots to do all the year round.

But Lightfoot made him wear his scarf always, because his soaking had given him a very weak throat, and as soon as he left off his scarf he caught a cold. He always remembers to put it on when he goes out of the burrow, and as it is a very bright orange, it is easy to see.

So if ever you see a rabbit playing on the hill-side, with an orange scarf tied round his throat, you'll know who he is – Benny! But don't tell Lucy, will you?

The Skittle-policeman

Angela had a box of funny skittle-men. Each man was different. One was a clown with a pointed hat. One was a soldier in red. Another was a sailor in a sailor suit, and a fourth was a policeman in blue. There were nine altogether, and in the box were three balls, red, white, and blue.

Angela used to stand the skittles up in two rows and then she and Nanny used to throw the balls at them and see who could knock down the most. It was great fun.

One day the skittle that looked like a policeman was hit seven times in one morning, and the seventh time a dreadful thing happened. His wooden nose came off! Yes, it did, and it rolled over the floor into a corner. The policeman-skittle was shocked and sad. Fancy having no nose! How dreadful he would look!

When Angela picked him up she squealed in dismay. "Oh, Nanny! He's lost his nose! I don't like him."

"Don't be silly," said Nanny. "I'll find his nose and stick it on for you again. Then he'll be all right."

But they couldn't find his nose, however hard they looked. Angela didn't like the policeman-skittle after that. She said he looked so horrid without a nose, and when Nanny had gone out of the room what do you think Angela did? She threw the skittle out of the window into the garden below! Wasn't it horrid of her?

Poor skittle! He fell into the wet grass and lay there, astonished and hurt. What was he going to do now!

All day long he lay there, and all day long it rained hard! When night came you wouldn't have known the skittle. All the paint had run off him, and he was just plain wood.

When the rain stopped and the moon shone out at night, the policeman-skittle sat up. He looked at himself. Goodness, what a sight he was! He felt his face. No nose! It was really dreadful. He wondered if he could find his nose if he went back to the nursery.

Somehow or other he climbed up the old apple tree by the wall and slipped in at the nursery window. The other toys were playing about on the floor very happily. When they saw the poor skittle-policeman with all his paint washed off him by the rain, they didn't know him.

"Who are you?" they shouted.

"I'm one of the skittle-men," said the policeman, humbly. "My nose was knocked off this morning and I've just come to see if I can find it."

"How awful you look without a nose!" said the sailor doll, unkindly. "And you've no paint at all."

"I can't help it," said the skittle, sadly. "It isn't my fault. It's Angela's fault."

"Well, we don't want you back here," said the toys to the poor washed-out skittle. "You look dreadful. Angela threw you away and you must stay away."

"All right," said the skittle, sighing. "Just let me find my nose and I'll go. But I think you're very horrid and unkind."

So they were, weren't they? Nobody helped the skittle to look for his nose, but he found it at last. He picked it up and went to the window.

"Goodbye," he said. "I'm sorry to leave you all."

"Goodbye," said the toys, and they turned their backs on him and began to play games again. The skittle slid down the apple tree and stood in the grass, wondering what to do.

He began to walk down the garden. He slipped under the hedge at the bottom and found himself in a field. He walked across it and came to a sloping hill-side.

The moon shone brightly. The skittle came to a little ring of toadstools, and then he heard a strange sound of grunting and panting. He looked to see what it was. To his great surprise he saw a small brownie tugging and pulling at the toadstools, trying his hardest to pull them up to carry away. But he couldn't drag the toadstools out of the ground, and at last he sat down on one, sighed heavily and said: "I shall never do it. I shall NEVER do it!"

The skittle felt sorry for the little creature. He walked up to one of the toadstools and tugged. Plip! It came away from the ground at once. In fact it gave way so suddenly that the skittle sat down hard on the ground and said "Oooh!" very loudly.

The brownie saw him and began to laugh. How he laughed! He laughed so much that the skittle began to laugh too.

"I say, I know I oughtn't to laugh at you when you were trying to help me," said the brownie, stopping at last. "But you looked so funny. Who are you?"

"I'm a skittle-policeman," said the skittle. "I've had my nose broken off, and Angela threw me out of the window because she didn't like me any more. Then the rain came and washed all my paint off me, so I haven't even a uniform on now. I'm afraid I look a dreadful creature."

"You do look rather odd," said the brownie, staring at him. "But you can't help it. I say, aren't you strong? Could you help me to move these toadstools, do you think?"

"Of course," said the skittle. "But why do you want to move them? They look all right just here."

"The silly things have grown in the wrong place," said the brownie. "They should have grown over there, where the magic bus stops – see, by that bush. They are seats for people waiting for the bus."

"Oh," said the skittle, looking in surprise at a bus that suddenly appeared round the bush. It wasn't much bigger than the toy bus in the nursery. It was full of mice, rabbits, and fairies. He stared and stared.

The bus drove off. The brownie began to tug hard at the toadstools again. "Let me do it," said the skittle, and he soon lifted two or three. The brownie carried them to the bus-stop and stood them there in a row. Presently little folk and three mice came along to wait for the bus. They were delighted to find the seats there and soon they were all full.

"It's very good of you to help me," said the brownie, when they had taken up all the toadstools and moved them to their right places. "I suppose I can't give you a cup of hot cocoa just to warm you up on this cold night?"

"Well, I'm quite warm," said the skittle. "But a cup of hot cocoa does sound very nice."

"Come on, then," said the brownie, and he took the skittle through a tiny door in the hill-side. Inside was a small and cosy room. A fire was burning at the end, and a kettle was singing on the hob. The brownie got out a cocoa tin and made some cocoa. Before long the skittle and the brownie were very friendly.

"It's a pity about your nose," said the brownie. "You would be nice-looking if you had a nose."

"Well, I've got it here," said the skittle. "But what's the good of a nose in your pocket?"

"Oh, you've got it, have you!" said the brownie. "Well, why not let me stick it on for you?"

"Oh, *could* you!" cried the skittle, delighted.

"Of course," said the brownie. "I can get some sticky glue from the buds of the chestnut tree, you know. The bees will go and collect enough for me. They are very clever at getting chestnut glue. Then I can stick your nose on for you."

That night the skittle slept at the brownie's house. He was happy, warm, and comfortable. This was better than living in the nursery with unkind toys and a little girl who threw you out of the window because you had lost your nose.

In the morning the sun shone. The brownie went outside and made a strange humming sound. Soon twelve brown-and-gold bees came flying up to hear what the brownie had to say.

"Collect me some sticky glue from the chestnut buds," he said. Off they flew. Soon they were back with the glue and they each put their sticky gift into a dish set ready for them. The brownie thanked them and went indoors. He heated the glue over the fire and then called the skittle to him. He took the little nose from him, smeared it with glue, and then stuck it firmly on the skittle's face. He stuck it on just a little bit crooked, but it didn't matter – it just made the skittle look comical and jolly.

"Ooh!" said the skittle, for the glue was hot. He stood still, quite brave, and in a few minutes there was his nose, firmly on his face again. How pleased he was!

"Many, many thanks," he said, looking at himself in a looking-glass. "That's fine! If only I could get myself a new coat of paint I should look just as grand as ever I did!"

"Well, perhaps we can manage that too," said the brownie, at once. "I know the elf who paints the bluebells in the spring, and if you don't mind rather a pale-blue for your uniform, I'm sure she would come and do it for you."

The skittle-policeman didn't know what to say, he was so pleased and grateful. Tears came into his eyes, and ran down his nose.

"I say, don't do that!" said the brownie, in alarm. "Your nose is only just stuck, you know! If you cry tears, it might come unstuck."

The skittle hurriedly dried his tears and smiled. "You are very good and kind to me," he said. "I would simply *love* a bluebell-coloured uniform."

So the next thing that happened was that they went to call on the elf who always painted the bluebells in May. She was pleased to see them and at once agreed to give the skittle a fine new blue uniform. She set to work that same day and you should have seen the policeman-skittle when she had finished. He looked simply beautiful.

"You look grand enough to go to Toytown and be the policeman there!" said the elf, looking at the skittle, very pleased with her painting. "The policeman there is old, and doesn't know how to deal with all the new traffic that's come in the last few years. You know, buses, trams, trains, motor-cars, and all that. Toytown used to be a peaceful sort of spot, but now it's all different."

The skittle-policeman listened, his eyes shining. How he had longed to be a real policeman and stand in the road with his hand out! But he had never been anything but a skittle, made to be knocked down and set up again.

"Oh," he said. "Oh! If only they'd let me try to do some proper

policeman's work in Toytown! How hard I would work! How careful I would be! I would see that no accident happened and that everything went at the right speed."

The brownie and the elf stared at one another in excitement.

"Come along!" they suddenly cried to the surprised skittle. "Come along! We'll get you the job! Oh, how pleased Toytown will be to have a new policeman!"

Soon the skittle found himself being dragged along to the bus at the corner. They all got in and in ten minutes' time they arrived at Toytown. The skittle felt quite at home when he saw teddy bears, dolls, and toy dogs walking about the streets. Everyone stared at him in admiration, for he really did look smart in his beautiful pale-blue uniform.

Well, he got the job, of course. The old policeman was only too glad to give it up.

The skittle walked proudly into the middle of the town, where the traffic was thickest, and five roads met. He held up his arm. Everything stopped at once. That was a proud moment for the skittle. He waved his hand. The cars and buses chugged onwards again.

Everyone came to look at the new policeman.

"What a beautiful uniform he has!" they cried. "What a lovely nose, just the weeniest bit crooked! Most unusual! How well he guides the traffic! He is a fine policeman, one to be proud of."

What do you think happened one day? A big motor-car came up, driven by a sailor doll. At the back were crowded a pack of skittle-men, two dolls, and a teddy bear – and they were all from Angela's nursery, where the skittle policeman had once lived!

"Honk, honk!" said the car, impatiently, for the sailor doll was in a hurry. The skittle-policeman knew that honk, and he looked round sharply. Ah, it was the toys he had once known! They were going too fast. He put up his hand to stop them. The sailor doll stopped, frowning. He was afraid of this policeman in his beautiful uniform. Suddenly the teddy bear gave a squeal.

"It's the policeman-skittle from the nursery, the one whose nose came off! Just look at him! Oooooh!"

The policeman turned round and looked at the toys. He didn't smile. He didn't blink an eye. He just looked at them very sternly.

The toys in the car went pale. They felt uncomfortable. They remembered how unkind they had been. The little doll burst into tears. The policeman-skittle said nothing at all. He waited until the road was clear and then he waved on the motor-car. The sailor doll was so nervous that he put on the brake instead of starting the car and the toys nearly fell out with the jerk.

"Come along, now, come along, now," said the skittle in his deepest voice. "Don't hold up the traffic."

The car at last went on. All the skittles stared back at the policeman in fear and admiration. What a grand fellow he was, to be sure! How sorry they were they had been unkind! Dear, dear, dear, what a mistake they had made! How they wished they were friends with him now!

But it was no use wishing. Once a chance of kindness is lost, it is gone for ever. The toys were very silent that day, and all of them were secretly making up their minds to be nicer in future.

As for the skittle-policeman, how he laughed when he told the brownie and the elf about the toys that night.

"You should have taken them all to prison," said the brownie, indignantly, for he was very fond of his skittle friend now.

"Oh, no," said the policeman. "I just looked at them like this – and they felt dreadful, I know they did!"

"You are a kind and clever fellow," said the elf, and she hugged the skittle. "Let's get married and then I can paint you a new uniform every year when I do the bluebells."

So they are married now, and very happy. And every day the skittle can be seen in Toytown, right in the middle of the street, stopping the traffic and waving it on just like any policeman in your own town. Wouldn't you like to see him? I would!

Tick-Tock's Tea-party

Tick-Tock the brownie lived with the enchanter Wind-Whistle, and kept his house neat and tidy for him. He cooked his meals, washed his clothes, and sometimes he helped Wind-Whistle with his spells. He was hard at work all day long, but he was very happy.

One afternoon there came a knock at the door and Tick-Tock went to open it. Outside stood the Princess of the Blue Hills and two of her court, come to visit the enchanter and take his advice.

It was just tea-time and Tick-Tock knew they would all stay to tea – and oh, dear me – there were no cakes at all, hardly any jam, and just a pinch of tea!

"Pray come inside!" said Tick-Tock, bowing low, for he knew his manners very well. The Princess came in, smelling very sweet and looking very lovely. Tick-Tock gave her and the ladies-in-waiting some chairs in the drawing room and went to tell Wind-Whistle of his royal visitor. All the time he was worrying about tea. What should he do for cakes and jam? You couldn't give royal princesses plain bread and butter – and goodness gracious, there was hardly any butter either! It was very worrying.

Wind-Whistle was pleased to hear of his royal visitor. He put on his best cloak at once and said to Tick-Tock: "Get tea ready. Lay it nicely."

"Oh, your highness, isn't it dreadful, there are no cakes, just a pinch of tea, hardly any jam, and not much butter!" said poor Tick-Tock.

"Well, go to the shops and get some," said the enchanter snappily.

"But they're shut this afternoon," said Tick-Tock. "It's early closing day!"

"Dear, dear, so it is," said the enchanter. "Well, never mind. Now listen carefully, Tick-Tock. Lay the table as usual, but place the butter-dish, the jam-dish, and cake-dishes empty on the table – empty, do you hear? Put no tea in the teapot, but fill it with boiling water. I have a mind to do a little magic for the Princess, and at the same time provide a good tea for her."

Tick-Tock listened open-mouthed. How exciting!

He hurried to do what he was told. He laid the table, put out empty butter, jam, and cake dishes, and filled the teapot with boiling water. Then he told the enchanter that everything was ready.

Wind-Whistle led the Princess and her ladies into the room where the tea was laid and bade them be seated. They were surprised to see nothing to eat.

"Madam, do you like Indian or China tea?" began the enchanter, holding up the teapot. Then he caught sight of the brownie Tick-Tock peeping in at the door to watch everything.

"Go to the kitchen!" he ordered. "And shut this door, Tick-Tock."

Poor Tick-Tock! He had so badly wanted to see everything. He shut the door and went to the kitchen – but in half a minute he was back again, peeping through the keyhole and listening to what the enchanter was saying!

"I'll have China tea," said the Princess.

"China tea, pour forth!" commanded the enchanter, and the Princess gave a scream of delight, for pale China tea poured from the teapot into her cup.

"I'd like Indian tea," said each of her ladies, and when Wind-Whistle said: "Indian tea, pour forth!" at once dark Indian tea poured into their cups.

"What sort of jam do you like?" asked Wind-Whistle.

"Strawberry, please," answered his three royal visitors.

"Strawberry jam, appear in the dish!" cried Wind-Whistle. Immediately a great heap of delicious jam appeared.

"And what cakes do you prefer?" asked the enchanter.

"Chocolate cakes for me!" cried the Princess in excitement.

"Cherry buns for me!" said the first lady.

"And ginger fingers for me!" begged the second lady.

"Chocolate cakes, appear!" commanded the enchanter, tapping a dish. "Cherry buns, come forth, ginger fingers, appear!"

Three dishes were suddenly full of the most delicious-looking cakes, and the ladies cried out in delight. Then the enchanter struck the butter-dish.

"Now, butter, where are you?" he cried. Golden butter at once gleamed in the dish. It was marvellous. Outside the door Tick-Tock listened to all this, and tried to see through the keyhole what was happening. It was most exciting.

After tea Wind-Whistle called Tick-Tock to him.

"I'm going to the Blue Hills with the Princess and her ladies," he said. "She needs my help. Look after my house and see that nothing goes wrong. And don't meddle with any magic or you will be sorry!"

By six o'clock Wind-Whistle and the ladies were gone and Tick-Tock was left alone. He finished up the cakes that were left from tea and enjoyed them very much. They were much nicer than any that were sold in the shops.

It was whilst he was eating the cakes that the naughty idea came to him. He clapped his hands for joy and danced round the kitchen.

"Why shouldn't I give a tea-party and make all the cakes and things appear!" he shouted. "I can wear the enchanter's magic cloak, and then all the things I say will come true too. Oh, how lovely! Won't I make everyone stare! My friends will think *I'm* an enchanter."

He sat down at once and wrote six notes to his friends. One

went to Big-Eyes, one to Little Feet, another to Pippity, the fourth to Gobo, and the last two to Tubby and Roundy the two fat brownies.

"Please come to a Magic Tea-party," he wrote to each of them. Then he licked up the envelopes and posted the letters. How excited he felt!

He had asked his friends for the next day. So he was very busy in the morning making the house tidy and putting fresh flowers on the tea-table. Then after his dinner he washed himself, did his hair nicely, laid the tea-table with empty plates and dishes, and at last went to put on the enchanter's magic cloak. It was embroidered with suns and moons and shone very brightly.

Tick-Tock walked about in front of the looking-glass in Wind-Whistle's bedroom and thought he looked really very grand.

"Won't I surprise everyone this afternoon!" he chuckled to himself. "Dear me! There's the clock striking half-past three! I must put the kettle on for tea."

He ran downstairs, nearly tripping over the cloak he wore, for it was much too big for him. He put the kettle on, and waited for his friends.

They all came together, looking very smart in their best clothes. They were most excited and crowded round Tick-Tock, asking him what a Magic Tea-party was.

"Wait and see, wait and see!" said Tick-Tock, laughing.

He led them into the dining-room, where tea was laid – but when they saw the empty dishes their faces grew long. Wasn't there going to be anything to eat?

"Wait and see, wait and see!" laughed Tick-Tock, again, running into the kitchen to fetch the kettle, which was now boiling.

His guests sat down round the table, and waited. Tick-Tock came back with the kettle. He was going to do better than the enchanter – he was going to make the cakes, jam, butter, and tea all appear at once!

"What sort of cakes and jam do you like?" he asked his guests. They all called out together.

"Gooseberry jam! Chocolate roll! Coconut buns! Cherry cake! Plum jam! Marmalade! Sponge fingers!"

"Right!" said Tick-Tock. He picked up the teapot, which he had filled with nothing but hot water, and then cried out loudly: "Tea, pour forth! Butter, appear! Gooseberry jam, plum jam, marmalade, where are you? Chocolate roll, coconut buns, cherry cake, sponge fingers, come forth!"

Then, to the enormous surprise of all his friends, the teapot poured tea into their cups, one after another, jam and marmalade began to come into the dishes, butter heaped itself up in another dish, and cakes fell into a pile on the rest of the dishes. It was perfectly marvellous!

"Wonderful!" cried Gobo.

"How do you do it!" shouted Tubby and Roundy.

"Goodness gracious!" cried the others.

"It's easy!" said Tick-Tock, pouring out his cup of tea last of all. "I'm quite a good magician, you know. I'm sure I could teach Wind-Whistle a lot."

A puzzled look came over the faces of the six guests as they watched the jam, butter, and cakes appearing in the dishes. They had been appearing for quite a while now, and the dishes were much too full. In fact the gooseberry jam was spilling on to the cloth.

"You ought to have put out bigger dishes," said Tubby to Tick-Tock. "Look, they aren't big enough for all the cakes and things."

But Tick-Tock was also feeling puzzled about something and didn't hear what Tubby said. The teapot had filled his cup, but when he set it down on the teapot stand, it didn't stay there. No, it hopped up into the air all by itself and began to pour tea into the milk-jug! It was most peculiar. Tick-Tock took hold of it and put it back on the tray. But as soon as he let go, up hopped the teapot into the air again and poured a stream of tea into the sugar-basin. It was most annoying.

"I say, Tick-Tock, the dishes aren't *big* enough, I tell you!" said Tubby, as he and the others watched the cakes spilling all over the table. "Shall we get some more?"

"No, just help yourselves and eat as much as you want to," said Tick-Tock, still busy with the obstinate teapot. "If you eat up the cakes there will soon be room for them on the dishes."

So the guests began eating – but, dear me, they couldn't eat nearly as fast as those cakes, jams, and butter appeared! Soon the tablecloth was in a dreadful mess, for the jam slid over the edge of the pot and dripped on to the table, and the butter flopped down too, while the marmalade was in big blobs all round its dish.

The cakes no longer fell on the dishes as they appeared out of the air, but bounced straight on to the table, scattering crumbs all over the place.

The guests were rather frightened, especially when they saw what trouble the teapot was giving poor Tick-Tock. But they said no more.

They ate steadily, though nothing really tasted very nice. Poor Tick-Tock could eat nothing for all the time he was trying to stop the teapot from pouring tea here, there, and everywhere.

At last it tore itself away from the frightened brownie and poured some tea down Gobo's neck!

"Ow!" squealed Gobo, jumping up in fright as the hot tea dripped down his collar. "Ow! Ooh! It's burnt me!"

He wiped the tea away with his handkerchief and began to cry.

"Hoo, hoohoo! I'm going home! This isn't a nice tea-party."

He ran out of the door and slammed it. The others looked at one another. The teapot moved towards Tubby, but he jumped out of the way.

"Good-bye, Tick-Tock," he said. "I must get home. I've some work to do."

"I must go with him," said Roundy, and the two brownies ran off in a hurry.

It wasn't long before the other guests went too. The magic was frightening them. It was all very well to have as many cakes as you wanted, but to see hundreds dropping on to the table was very peculiar. They felt sure something had gone wrong.

Tick-Tock was very unhappy and rather frightened. What had happened? Hadn't he done the magic just the same as Wind-Whistle? Why wouldn't everything stop appearing? Why didn't that horrid teapot stop pouring?

Tick-Tock looked round the table in despair. What a mess! Look at all the jam and marmalade! Look at those cakes, not even bothering to fall on the dishes any more! Look at the butter all over the place! And look at that perfect nuisance of a teapot pouring tea on the carpet now! Whatever was he to do?

Poor Tick-Tock! He couldn't do anything. He had started a magic that he couldn't stop. The teapot suddenly stopped pouring tea on the carpet and playfully poured some on Tick-Tock's beautiful cloak. He cried out in dismay.

"Oh! Look what you've done to the enchanter's best cloak! Oh, what a mess! Whatever will he say? Oh, my goodness me, I must go and sponge off the tea at once!"

Tick-Tock rushed upstairs to the bathroom. He took a sponge and began to sponge the tea stain on the cloak. He was dreadfully afraid the enchanter would see it, and what would he say then? Oh, dear, dear, why ever had Tick-Tock meddled with magic when he had been told not to?

It took a long time to get the tea stain out of the cloak, but at last it was done. Tick-Tock hung the cloak over a chair to dry and was just going downstairs when he heard someone shouting from outside the house. He stuck his head out of the window to see what the matter was.

Out of doors stood Gobo, and he was shouting at the top of his voice.

"Hi, Tick-Tock! Are you all right? There are a lot of funny things happening down here! Look!"

Tick-Tock looked – and out of the front door he saw a stream of tea flowing! Yes, really, it was running down the path! Mixed with it was butter, jam, marmalade, and cakes of all kinds, bobbing up and down in the stream.

"Oooooh!" screamed Tick-Tock, and ran downstairs in a hurry. Well! I couldn't tell you what the dining-room looked like. It was a foot deep in tea, to begin with, for the teapot was still pouring away merrily. And then the cakes! Well, there were hundreds and hundreds of them. The jam and marmalade and butter were all mixed up together, and still more and more things were dropping down into the room.

Tick-Tock waded in. The teapot at once poured some tea on his nose and he gave a cry of pain, for it was hot. Whatever was he to do? This was dreadful.

"Can't you stop the things coming and coming and coming?" shouted Gobo, who was really very sorry for his friend. "You made them start."

"I know," sobbed Tick-Tock. "But I thought they would stop by themselves and they haven't. If only Wind-Whistle was here!"

Then Gobo gave a shout and pointed up the street. "Here he comes!" he cried. "He's come home sooner than you thought!"

So he had. Poor Tick-Tock! He didn't know whether to be glad or sorry. Wind-Whistle strode up the road and when he came to his house and saw the stream of tea pouring out, mixed with jam and cakes, he was most astonished. He stared at it in amazement, whilst poor Tick-Tock tried to stammer all about it.

"What! You dared to meddle with magic when I told you not to!" shouted the enchanter in anger. "You wore my magic cloak! How dare you?"

"Oh, please, your highness, forgive me!" wept the brownie, as white as a sheet. "I just thought I would give a tea-party like you did. It looked so easy. But nothing would stop. It just went on and on. The teapot is still pouring in the dining-room."

The enchanter waded through the stream of tea and looked in at the dining-room door. What a dreadful sight! He frowned in anger. Then he clapped his hands sharply three times and said: "Illa rimmytooma lippitty crim!" These words were so magic that Tick-Tock trembled to hear them. But at the sound of them the teapot at once stopped its pouring and put itself in the sink to be washed up. The cakes stopped falling from the air, and so did the jam, marmalade, and butter.

But the dreadful mess remained. Tick-Tock looked at it in despair.

"Aren't you going to make all this mess go too?" he asked his master.

"No, *you're* going to make that go!" said Wind-Whistle, sternly. "Get brushes, cloths, soap and water, Tick-Tock, and clear it up. It will keep you busy."

Tick-Tock went away howling. The mess would take him days to clear up. But it was his own fault, he shouldn't have meddled with magic. He never would again, never!

Wind-Whistle forgave Tick-Tock, when the house was clean and tidy again. But when he wants to tease the little brownie, he says: "Would you like another tea-party, Tick-Tock, some day?"

But Tick-Tock shakes his head and cries: "No, no, no. Never again!"

The Surprise Party

There was once a brown teddy bear who was always miserable. You should have seen him! He went about with a long face, his whiskers drooping and his ears down. Nobody knew what was the matter with him, they just knew that he was miserable, and that it didn't seem to be any good to try to cheer him up.

As for the teddy bear himself, he was a foolish fellow. He thought that nobody liked him or wanted him. When he saw the other toys laughing and joking together, giving each other presents, and helping one another, he pulled a longer face than ever. He thought it was too bad that they left him out of everything.

And the toys thought that it was too bad that he wouldn't join in anything – so you see things got worse and worse, and soon the teddy bear went and moped in a corner all day and wouldn't even answer when he was spoken to.

The toys laughed about it at first – and then, because they were kind-hearted, they began to worry about the teddy bear. They sent to the pixie who lived in the pansy bed under the nursery window and asked him for his advice. He was old and very wise.

He peeped in at the window and saw the brown bear moping in a corner, looking very lonely and miserable. He shook his head and thought for a long while.

"I'll tell you the best medicine for him," he said at last. "Give him a great big surprise! That's the best cure for anyone who's moping."

"What sort of surprise?" asked the French doll.

"Oh, any kind, so long as it's nice," said the pixie. "That ought to cure him. Don't let him guess what we're doing, though, or that will spoil it."

Well, the toys sat in a corner together and talked about it. What kind of surprise could they give the teddy bear? They really couldn't think of anything!

Then the yellow duck suddenly thought of something. "Why," she said, flapping her plush wings in delight, "I know! It's the teddy bear's birthday on Saturday. He came from the same shop as I did, and I quite well remember him telling me one day when his birthday was. Couldn't we give him a birthday party? That would be a wonderful surprise!"

All the toys thought the duck's plan was a very good one. So they began to think what they should do.

"I will make the teddy bear a fine blue sash," said the French doll, who was very clever with her fingers. "He will like that to wear at his party."

"And I will make some chocolate buns on the little stove in the doll's house," said the sailor doll, who was really a very good cook.

"I'll make some toffee!" cried the clockwork mouse.

"Sh!" said everyone. "The teddy bear will hear you! Remember, it must all be a great surprise!"

The teddy bear heard all the toys whispering together in the corner, and he felt more out of things than ever. What were they whispering about now?

"I expect they are saying horrid things about me!" said the bear sulkily. "Oh, dear, how I wish I didn't live in this horrid nursery, with all these horrid toys always whispering horrid things about me. I've a good mind to run away!"

The toys went on with their plans for the party. They decided to build a big house of the pink and blue toy bricks, and to hold the party there. Besides the chocolate buns there should be ginger fingers and sugar biscuits. The pixie promised to bring them some honey lemonade to drink. There were plenty of cups, saucers and plates in the dolls' tea-set for the toys to use. What fun it would be!

They would have games afterwards, and the teddy bear should choose them. The clockwork train promised that if it were wound up it would give the bear six rides round the nursery, which was really a very great treat indeed, for usually the toy train was lazy and wouldn't give a ride to anyone at all!

Then there were presents for the bear. There was a fine walking-stick. It was really a pencil with a curved end like a handle, and it belonged to the children whose nursery the toys lived in. But they had thrown the pencil away because it wouldn't write properly. The toys found it and thought it would make a fine walking-stick. So they polished it up and made it shine beautifully.

Then there was a little red and yellow brooch that had come out of a Christmas cracker. It was very pretty and the toys felt sure the bear would like it. There was also a pair of small blue shoes, too large for the smallest doll and too small for the other dolls. They would fit the teddy bear very well, the toys thought.

Nicest of all there was a wonderful little chair, made by the pixie outside, out of bent hazel and willow twigs woven together. That was really a fine surprise.

All the toys were to be in their best clothes. Those that hadn't best clothes, or no clothes at all were to wash themselves well and brush their fur or hair. The party was to begin at four o'clock with a song made up by the sailor doll especially for the teddy bear.

The toys were more excited that week than they had ever been before. What whispering there was! What planning. What laughing and joking!

The teddy bear couldn't for the life of him make out what was happening. He tried to listen to the whispering but all he heard was "the party". Then he was more unhappy than ever because he felt sure the toys were going to have a party without him.

"They don't want me," said the poor foolish bear. "They're going to have a party and keep me out of it. The horrid, nasty things!"

Now the toys didn't want the teddy bear to see them building the brick house, or changing into their best clothes on Saturday afternoon in case he guessed their secret. So they decided to ask him to go out for a little walk, and then, while he was gone, they could get everything ready for his party.

So the sailor doll went to him on Saturday at two o'clock, and said kindly: "Teddy, go for a little walk until four o'clock. It is a sunny afternoon and it will do you good."

The teddy bear went red with rage. So they were going to get him out of the way, were they, while they were having their party! They were going to eat everything up! They weren't even going to let him see the party!

He rushed out of the door, with angry tears in his boot-button eyes. It was too bad! He'd run away! Yes, he would!

Off he went down the garden path. He walked and walked and walked. All the time he thought angrily about the toys.

"I *will* run away!" he said to himself. "Yes, I will! But first I'll go back and tell the toys just what I think of them. I'll tell them how horrid they are – how unkind – how selfish! I'll go straight back now and tell them!"

Back he went to the nursery, quite determined to say some very horrid things. It was just four o'clock when he arrived; the toys had finished getting ready for the party, and were standing in a line ready to sing the song that the sailor doll had made up for them.

The bear stamped into the nursery and glared round at the toys.

"I've just come back to tell you what a lot of nast–" he began –

but he couldn't finish because at a sign from the sailor doll the toys opened their mouths and their beaks and began to sing very loudly:

"Here's a welcome hearty
To your birthday party.
Welcome, birthday-bear,
Hurry up and share
In our games and fun
Till your birthday's done!"

Then they stopped, took a long breath and shouted: "Many happy returns of the day, bear! Many happy returns of the day!"

They crowded round him shaking him by the paw, and the little pink rabbit gave him a hug!

The teddy bear was so surprised that at first he couldn't think what to say.

"But – but – but – is it my birthday?" he asked.

"Yes!" shouted the toys. "And we hadn't forgotten it! We've been having secrets about it all the week. We were so afraid you'd guess. *Did* you guess?"

"Oh, no," said the bear, going quite red to think of all the horrid things he had thought. "I didn't guess for a minute."

"Here's a nice blue birthday sash!" said the French doll. She wound it round his fat little body and tied it in a big bow. He looked beautiful.

"And here's a brooch – and a pair of blue shoes – and a fine walking-stick!" cried everyone, giving the surprised bear the presents. The shoes fitted him beautifully, and the brooch looked lovely just under his chin. As for the walking-stick he was as proud of it as he could be. Dear me, could all this be a dream? How lovely! What a silly bear he had been!

They had tea in the splendid brick house. The biscuits, cakes and sweets were most delicious, and the honey lemonade was so nice that the bear had five glasses of it and felt rather like a balloon at the end. But he was so happy that he didn't mind anything.

Then they had games, and after that the bear rode in the clockwork train six times round the nursery. That was lovely. Then he was presented with the chair that the pixie had made for him, and he was so surprised that he could hardly sit down in it! But he did, at last, and it was exactly the right size for him. His very own chair! How proud and pleased he was. He wanted to thank the pixie, so the little creature was called and came in to eat a chocolate bun.

He looked at the bear with a twinkle in his eye.

"Do you know," he said solemnly, "I saw a horrid little bear this afternoon, going along muttering the nastiest things about dolls, and sailor dolls, and ducks, and every sort of toy."

The teddy bear looked as red as a tomato. How dreadful! The pixie must have seen him going for that walk!

"But it couldn't have been you, could it?" said the pixie, his bright eyes twinkling more than ever, as he looked at the bear.

"It must have been a foolish, sulky, stupid little bear who didn't know what he was talking about."

"Yes, it was," said the teddy bear humbly. "Well, pixie, that little bear will never be so foolish again. I know the toys are my friends, and I will be a friend to them. They have given me a lovely birthday, and I will never forget it. It was a wonderful surprise."

"Ah!" said the pixie wisely, smiling round at the listening toys. "A surprise is a fine thing isn't it, toys? It's a splendid cure for the mopes – and don't you forget it!"

The teddy bear never forgot it. He is always planning lovely surprises for everyone, and he never *thinks* of sulking in a corner now!

The Enchanted Doll

Mollie had a pretty doll called Angela, whom she loved very much indeed. She played with Angela all day long, and the only thing she wished was that Angela could talk and walk, instead of just lying or sitting perfectly still, and staring at Mollie with wide-open blue eyes.

"I can pretend you talk to me, and I can pretend you run about and play," said Mollie, "but you don't really and truly – and it *would* be such fun, Angela dear, if just for once in a way you would really come alive!"

But Angela just sat and stared, and didn't move a finger or say a word! It was most disappointing, for she really was a nice doll, and Mollie felt quite certain that if only she *could* talk and walk, she would be a good companion to have. Mollie had no brothers or sisters, so she was often lonely. That was why she played so much with Angela.

One day a very strange thing happened to Mollie. She took her doll for a walk in Pixie Wood, and it happened there. Mollie had never seen any pixies or anything at all exciting in Pixie Wood, although it had such a lovely name. It was just like an ordinary wood.

But today it seemed a little different. The trees seemed closer together, as if they were nodding to one another, and whispering about something. The sun couldn't get in between the branches, and the wood was dim and rather mysterious. Mollie took Angela by the hand and walked her over the grass, talking to her. Her doll's pram was broken and had gone to be mended, which was why Angela was not riding in it as usual.

Mollie walked on through the wood – and then she suddenly stopped short. She saw something most surprising in the wood! It was a tiny pram, a little smaller than a doll's pram, and it shone like pure gold. It had a little white hood with a silver fringe hanging down, and the pram cover was white too, with gold embroidery on it. It really was very beautiful.

"Whatever is a doll's pram doing here in the middle of the wood?" wondered Mollie. "I haven't seen any other children about. I wonder if they've left their pram here and are playing hide-and-seek or something. I'll cuckoo to them and see where they are. Perhaps they would let me play with them."

So she called loudly: "Cuckoo! Cuckoo! Where are you? Can I play with you?"

But there was no answer. The trees seemed to lean closer to one another, and all the leaves whispered again. Mollie looked all round and ran here and there, but it was no use at all – she couldn't see any children.

She looked at the lovely little pram. It was the nicest she had ever seen. How pretty Angela would look if she were tucked up in it and taken for a ride! Mollie went over to the pram and turned back the cover. There was no doll inside – but would you believe it, there was a little bottle there full of milk!

"But this pram can't belong to a *real* baby! It can't!" cried Mollie, in astonishment. "It's too small. Oh! I wonder – I just wonder if it belongs to a pixie! It would be just right for a pixie baby. Oh, how lovely! I wish, I wish, I wish I could see a real pixie baby riding in that dear little pram!"

Mollie waited for a little while to see if anyone came, but nobody did. Then a thought slid into her mind – would it matter if she put Angela into the pram and just wheeled her about for five minutes? Angela must be tired with her long walk, and really, she would look perfectly sweet in that pram! It wouldn't spoil the pram.

So Mollie picked up Angela and put her into the pram. She sat her down firmly, strapped her in, and set the soft pillow up behind her so that she could sit up comfortably. Then she tucked the white cover round her and began to wheel her about. How pretty Angela looked in the pixie pram! It was most exciting to wheel her about in it.

Mollie gave Angela a ride for a few minutes and then she thought she saw a little pointed face peeping at her from behind a tree.

"Who's there?" she called. "Come and see Angela in this dear little pram, pixie!"

There was no answer – so Mollie left the pram and ran to the tree to see if the pixie really was peeping there. But, wasn't it disappointing, there was no one there at all, except a scurrying rabbit with a white bobtail!

Mollie turned back to the pram, and oh dear me, what a shock she got! The pram was running away! Yes, it really was! It was wheeling off all by itself, between the trees, as fast as ever it could!

"Oh! Oh! Come back, come back!" shouted Mollie. "Angela, Angela! Oh, please, pram, do come back! Don't take Angela away!"

But the pram hurried on. Mollie wondered if an invisible fairy was wheeling it, or whether the pram was a magic one that could go by itself. Oh, why, why had she put Angela in it! She ran after the hurrying pram as fast as ever she could, shouting as she went. The pram went faster and faster. It was dreadful. Mollie caught sight of the doll's face. It was full of horror and fear, and the little girl was sorry for her doll. She must, she really must, catch that pram!

The pram turned a corner by some thick bushes, and disappeared from sight. Mollie panted after it, but alas, when she reached the bushes, she could no longer see the pram. It was quite gone!

Mollie ran wildly about, and began to cry when she could not see the pram anywhere.

"Where have you gone, Angela?" she shouted. "Can't you call and tell me?"

But there was no answer. Angela had disappeared with the pram.

Mollie sat down and cried bitterly. It was dreadful to lose her doll like that. She did love her so much.

Presently she felt a little hand on her shoulder and a high, twittering voice said: "What's the matter? Would you mind getting up? You are sitting on my front door."

Mollie looked up in surprise. She saw a tiny creature by her, with long, pointed wings, pointed ears, and pointed shoes. It was smaller even than Angela, her doll, and was looking at her with big green eyes.

"Are you a pixie?" asked Mollie, in astonishment. "How small you are! Am I really on your front door? I'm so sorry."

She got up, and saw that she was sitting on a small yellow trap-door, sunk deeply into the ground. The pixie opened it and then looked at Mollie.

"Why are you crying?" he said.

Mollie told him all about the little pram she had found, and how it had run off with her doll.

"Oh, that pram belongs to Mother Dimity, the old woman who lives in a shoe," said the pixie at once. "She is very forgetful, you know, and leaves it about everywhere! If she goes home without it, she whistles for it and it goes to her of its own accord."

"Well, it's taken my doll too," said Mollie, beginning to cry again. Her tears fell in at the pixie's trap-door and he frowned.

"Please don't do that," he said. "You are making my home all damp. Why are you crying now? You can easily go and find your doll. Mother Dimity will give her back if you ask her."

"Where does she live?" asked Mollie.

"In the Shoe," said the pixie, getting into his trap-door home. "Knock at the Big Oak Tree six times, go down the steps, find a boat to take you on the Underground River, and then ask the Wizard Who Grows Toadstools where the Shoe is. He is sure to know, because the Old Woman is his sister."

"Thank you," said Mollie, getting up. The pixie said goodbye and shut his trap-door with a bang. Mollie looked round for the Big Oak Tree. There were a great many oak trees around, and they all seemed about the same size to the little girl. She chose one that looked a little bigger than the others and knocked six times. Nothing happened at all. She knocked again. Still nothing happened.

"It can't be the right tree," said Mollie, disappointed. She looked round again – and then she saw the biggest oak she had ever seen in her life! It was a real monster, towering up into the sky, and as big and round as a summer house!

"That's the one!" thought Mollie, and she ran over to it. She knocked on the trunk sharply six times – rat-tat-tat-tat-tat-tat! Then there came a creaking noise, and to her great delight a small door swung open in the tree and she saw that a narrow flight of steps led downwards towards the roots.

Her heart beat fast. This was a wonderful adventure! She slipped through the door, which at once shut with a bang, and began to go down the steps. It was rather dark, but small lanterns which hung here and there gave a little light. Mollie went down for a long way.

She thought she must have climbed down quite a hundred steps when she came to a wide passage, with doors on every side. She looked at them. They all had names on, or messages written on little cards.

One card said: "Ring, don't knock." Another said: "Knock, don't ring." The next door had a card that said: "Don't knock or ring," and the fourth one said: "I am not at home yesterday or tomorrow."

Mollie thought that was strange, and she giggled. The names were strange too. "Mister Woozle" was on one card, and "Dame High-go Quick" was on another. Mollie read a third one, "Little Jiggy-jig", and she was just wondering whatever he could be like when his door flew open and someone rushed out and nearly knocked her down. It was Little Jiggy-jig himself!

He was a funny fellow, with small wings, rabbit's ears and a funny habit of jigging up and down. "Sorry!" he said to Mollie. "Didn't see you there!"

He was just about to rush away when Mollie caught hold of his arm. "Wait a minute," she said. "Could you please tell me if I am on the right way to the Underground River. "

"Yes, yes," said Little Jiggy-jig, jerking his arm away impatiently. "First to the right and left and then straight on round the corner."

"But how can I go to the right and left at once, and how can anyone go straight round a corner!" called Mollie, indignantly. The only answer she got was a chuckle, and Little Jiggy-jig disappeared into the darkness of the passage. Mollie felt cross. She went straight on, and at last heard a noise of lapping water.

"That must be the Underground River," she thought, pleased. "Now to find a boat!"

She soon came to the river. It was hung with fairy lights of all colours and looked very pretty. There were plenty of boats on the side of it, but none of them had oars in them. Mollie looked about for someone to row her down the river, but she could see no one.

"Isn't there anyone here?" she shouted. Then a little head came poking out of a funny little ticket-office Mollie had not noticed.

"Yes, I'm here, and you're here too," said the person in the ticket-office. Mollie went up and saw that it was a grey rabbit with a collar round its neck, and a tie flowing down, very neatly knotted.

"Good morning," said Mollie. "I want a boat."

"Here's your ticket, then," said the rabbit, handing her a very chewed-looking piece of cardboard.

"Where's the boatman?" asked Mollie.

"Nowhere," said the rabbit. "There isn't one."

"Then how can I go in a boat?" asked Mollie.

"Get in it yourself, silly," said the rabbit.

"Don't be rude," said Mollie. "It's no use taking a boat if you haven't got oars, is it? Silly yourself!"

"Now who's being rude!" said the rabbit. "You are being very simple, little girl. Why do you want to take a boat? Why not let the boat take *you*?"

Mollie glared at the rabbit, and then walked up to one of the boats. She chose a blue one, dotted with gold stars, and got into it. At once the boat glided off by itself.

"Good morning, good afternoon and good evening!" shouted the rabbit, but Mollie didn't answer. She thought he was rather silly.

The boat shot on down the river, and after a little while it left the underground darkness and came out into the open air. Mollie blinked in the bright sunshine, but she was very glad indeed to be in the light again. The boat sped on and on, and Mollie watched the strange folk walking in the flowery fields, and saw with surprise that the animals were dressed up like human beings.

The boat went on, rocking gently. Mollie suddenly saw a curious field, with a strange-looking old man waving a stick about in the middle of it. He was surrounded by toadstools of all sizes, colours, and shapes, and she knew that he must be the Wizard Who Grows Toadstools.

"Stop, stop!" she cried to the boat. It stopped at once and headed to the bank. Mollie patted it, said thank you and then jumped out. She went to the old wizard, who didn't see her at first and almost knocked her over with his waving stick, which the little girl now saw was a silver wand.

"Please," she said. "I've come to ask you where your sister, the old woman who lives in a shoe, is. I want to go and speak to her."

"You'll find her on the other side of that hill," said the wizard, waving his wand violently, and nearly catching Mollie in the eye with it. "Look out! You are standing just where my next toadstool is growing!"

Mollie felt the earth pushing up under her feet and fell over. A big toadstool appeared through the ground and grew high and

broad. It was covered with big red spots. Mollie sat on the ground and watched it in amazement. Then she felt the earth moving just under her again, and at once she was shot up high on another growing toadstool.

"Well, really," said the wizard, in disgust, "how you do get in the way, to be sure! Mind where you tread as you go through the field. There are toadstools growing everywhere today, for I have a very large order for them from the King himself, who wants three hundred for stools for his next party."

Mollie ran out of the field as quickly as she could, and made her way to the hill in the distance. She climbed it, and as soon as she came to the top she saw the Shoe. It was an enormous shoe, and it had windows and doors in it and a smoking chimney at the top. Mollie thought it looked lovely. She ran down to it, and at once she was surrounded by a crowd of small pixie children, not so big as she was, with pointed faces, pointed ears, and short wings.

"Who are you? Where do you come from?" they cried in excitement. "Have you come to see our new child?"

"Look, our new little girl is in bed! You can see her through the window!" said a tiny pixie, taking Mollie's hand and leading her to a window that looked into the Shoe house. Mollie peeped in – and whatever do you think she saw? She saw a bedroom in the Shoe, with many little white beds in it, and in one of them, the bed nearest to the window, lay Angela, her own little doll!

"Do you see that new little girl?" said the pixie. "Well, she came in today in Mother Dimity's pram, and do you know, she is very ill, poor thing! She can't talk, she can't eat, she can't drink, she can't even blink her eyes! Isn't it dreadful! I've never seen a little girl like that before, have you?"

"That isn't a little girl at all, that's my doll!" cried Mollie.

"A doll!" said the pixie children, crowding round Mollie. "What's a doll? We don't know what a doll is."

"Well, a doll is – a doll is – well, that's what a doll is!" said Mollie, pointing to where Angela lay on the little bed.

"But can't the poor thing move or talk at all?" asked the pixies in surprise.

"Of course not," said Mollie. "I'm going in to get Angela. Poor darling, she must feel so frightened!"

She ran in at the door of the big Shoe, and bumped into the Old Woman.

"Now then, gently, gently!" said Mother Dimity. "You'll frighten the new little girl, rushing about like that. I've just given her some very strong magic medicine to make her come alive again."

"She never has been alive!" cried Mollie. "She's my doll!"

"Your doll!" said the Old Woman. "Doll! Oh, I remember once seeing a doll in the world of boys and girls. Dear, dear me, so that's a doll, is it? Why, I thought it was a little girl that was ill, and so I've given her some stuff to make her walk and talk. I'm really very sorry indeed."

"But, do you mean to say that Angela will soon walk and talk?" cried Mollie.

"Of course," said Mother Dimity. "Look – she is blinking her eyes now! Perhaps I had better make her go back into a doll again."

"No, please don't," said Mollie at once. She ran to Angela and looked at her. Wonder of wonders, the little doll was opening and shutting her eyes and she suddenly looked at Mollie and smiled a wide smile, showing all her pretty teeth.

"Hello, Mollie," she said. "I've often wanted to talk to you, and now I can!"

Mollie watched her in amazement. Angela threw back the covers and jumped out of bed. She danced round the room in joy and then ran up to Mollie. She hugged the little girl's legs, and Mollie lifted her up into her arms. She was so pleased to have Angela back, walking and talking, that the tears ran down her cheeks in joy.

"Oh, what fun we'll have together now!" she cried, hugging her doll to her. "We can talk to one another, and play all kinds of games."

"But you mustn't let anyone but yourself know," said Mother Dimity at once. "If you do, the magic will go, and Angela will be an ordinary doll again."

"Oh, I won't tell anyone at all!" said Mollie, happily. "Come on, Angela, we'll go home again now. It must be getting late."

She put the little doll on the ground and Angela took her hand. Then, walking like a real person, she trotted beside Mollie, saying goodbye to all the pixie children.

Mother Dimity showed them a short way home, and they arrived there just in time for dinner. Mollie put Angela in her cot, and told her to be sure not to move if anyone came in, and she promised.

And now Mollie is as happy as the day is long, for she has a real, live doll to play with her, and they *do* have some fine games together.

"Really," Mollie's mother often says, "you might think that doll was alive, the way Mollie plays with her all day long!"

And then Mollie smiles a big smile – but she doesn't say a word! She has a wonderful secret to keep and she keeps it very well!

Poor Old Scarecrow!

There was once an old scarecrow who stood in the middle of a farmer's field. The farmer had made the scarecrow, and really, he looked very life-like. He had a turnip for a head, with eyes and mouth scooped out, and a piece of stick for a nose. He had an old bowler hat on his turnip head. Round his neck was a red scarf full of holes.

He wore a dirty old coat of the farmer's and a pair of trousers so ragged that, really, it was a marvel they hung together. But they did. He had two sticks for legs and two sticks for arms, and that was all there was of him.

He stood in the field on the sloping hillside, and looked in front of him all day long. The birds were not a bit afraid of him except when the wind blew his coat and scarf about. Then they thought he was alive and flew off, frightened.

"Silly creatures!" thought the scarecrow, scornfully. "Frightened by a bit of flapping in the breeze. Oh, dear me, what a life this is! Nothing ever happens. All I see are the foolish birds and a lolloping rabbit or two. I want someone to talk to. There are many things I think about as I stand here all day long. Surely I am not too ugly for other creatures to speak to me. What about the pixies in the hedge? Why don't they pass the time of day with me sometimes? Are they too high and mighty?"

The pixies were not too high and mighty, nor were the goblins who lived in the caves along the hillside. But they were afraid to visit the scarecrow. You see, he really was so ugly, so dirty, so ragged! So they kept away from him, and even when he beckoned to them with his stick-like hand they pretended not to see him.

Now one night something very exciting happened to the scarecrow. It was like this. He stood out there in the middle of the field, yawning and bored. It was cold and he was lonely. Only a rabbit had come near him that day, and he really was longing to talk to someone.

So when he saw two strange figures walking over his field, he was very much excited.

"They are coming to visit me!" he thought. "At last I shall have someone to talk to! How marvellous!"

But when the two people came nearer in the pale moonlight the scarecrow saw that they were almost as ugly as he was! They were witches, long and lean, bony and bent.

"Let us talk here," said one witch to the other. "No one will hear us, in the middle of this lonely field. We will sit down beside the scarecrow and whisper our secret plans."

"What a scarecrow it is, too!" said the second witch, scornfully, looking the poor scarecrow up and down. "Turnip head and turnip brains! Silly, gaping thing!"

The scarecrow was so hurt and surprised at these unkind words that he couldn't think of anything at all to say. He just stood and gaped all the more, and he felt as if his scarf was choking him.

The witches took no more notice of him. They sat down on the cold earth and began to whisper.

Now the scarecrow's ears were not much to look at, but they were very sharp, so he could hear every word that was said. And very strange was the thing that the witches talked about on that moonlit night.

"The Princess comes this way tomorrow night," whispered the first witch. "She will only be attended by two fairies, and she will be in her rabbit-carriage."

"Then we will lie in wait for her under the blackberry hedge over there," whispered the other witch. "We will take her prisoner and throw the fairies with her into the nearest holly bush."

Both the witches laughed at this. The scarecrow was so amazed at what he heard that his hat fell off. Both the witches jumped up in alarm, and when they saw it was only the scarecrow's hat that had made them jump, they stared at the scarecrow angrily. The first witch picked up his hat and jammed it down so hard on his turnip head that it went over one of his eyes so that he could hardly see. But he didn't say a word. No, he knew better than that!

"No one knows of our plan," said the first witch. "Meet me here tomorrow night, friend, before the moon rises, and we will go to the hedge to lie in wait for the Princess."

They went silently down the hill together, their pointed hats showing up in the moonlight, two strange and ugly figures. The scarecrow blinked his turnip eyes and thought hard about what he had heard.

He wondered who the Princess was who was coming that way the next night. So when he saw a small rabbit venturing into the field to eat a few shoots, he called to him in his funny woodeny voice:

"Rabbit! There is something important I must say to you. Come nearer."

The rabbit looked at the scarecrow in alarm. He lolloped just a little nearer and cocked his long ears up at the scarecrow.

"Don't flap your coat at me," he said, "or I shall run away."

"Don't be silly," said the scarecrow impatiently. "*I* don't flap it. It's only the wind. Listen, rabbit. Who is the Princess who is coming this way tomorrow night?"

"It's the Princess Peronel of Pixieland," said the rabbit in surprise. "However did you hear that news, scarecrow? Why, we thought only the rabbits knew, because two bunnies that pull the carriage told us. Don't you tell anyone, now!"

"There's no need to," said the scarecrow. "Lots of people seem to know! There were two witches here just now, and they said that . . ."

But the rabbit didn't wait to hear any more. At the mention of the word "witches" he was off like a shot! Witches! Tails and whiskers, to think that he was out on a night that witches chose! Ooh!

The scarecrow looked at the running rabbit angrily. *Now* what was he to do? Just as he was telling the rabbit, so that he might be able to lollop off and warn the Princess, the silly little creature must needs run away as if a hundred dogs were after him!

"Hi!" called the scarecrow, in despair. "Hi! Come back! I've got something very important to say."

But the rabbit had disappeared into a hole and had warned all the other rabbits that witches were about. So not a single rabbit showed itself again that night, and the scarecrow shouted himself hoarse.

He began to get alarmed. Just suppose he couldn't get help in time? Just suppose the little Princess Peronel should really be taken prisoner by those two horrid witches! Just suppose – but the scarecrow really couldn't suppose any more.

When the sun rose, the birds came flying into the field. "Perhaps if I call and beckon to them they will listen to what I have to say," thought the scarecrow.

So he began to call to the birds in his hoarse, woodeny voice, and he flapped his arm-sleeves about to beckon them and waggled his trouser legs.

But, dear me, the birds came no nearer – no, they were frightened, and flew away at once screeching: "The scarecrow is alive today! Beware! Don't go near him! He'll be walking down the field next!"

The scarecrow listened to their calls, and then a sudden thought came to him. He never *had* tried to walk, but just supposing he could? If he managed to walk down to the rabbit-holes he could give the warning easily then. He could shout it down the burrows.

Now, you know, scarecrows are so stiff that they cannot usually put one leg in front of another. But our scarecrow began to try. He had all the day in front of him, so he had plenty of time.

First he tried to pull a leg out of the ground. How he tried! How he tugged, how he pulled!

It was no good. He couldn't seem to move his leg at all. The farmer had driven the stick-legs firmly into the ground, and it was more than the poor scarecrow could do to move them. He was really in despair.

He stood gazing in front of him, feeling hot and out of breath, when he saw a peculiar thing. Not far from him he saw a little mound of earth rising. Then another. Then another. Whatever could that be?

He soon knew. A little velvet mole came peeping out of the ground, but when he spied the scarecrow nearby he gave a squeal of fright and made as if he would dive back into the earth again.

"Mole, mole, don't go," begged the scarecrow. "I won't hurt you. I really won't. Listen, two witches are planning to take the Princess Peronel prisoner tonight. Will you go and warn the rabbits?"

"What is a witch?" asked the mole. "And what is a Princess? Are they things to eat? I should like to hear of some nice new beetles to hunt for."

"No, they're not things to eat," said the scarecrow, in despair. "Oh, you silly little mole, never mind what they are. Just go and give my message to the rabbits. It's important."

"Nothing's important but food," said the mole. "I'm sorry, scarecrow, but I can't go out of my way to tell a silly message I don't understand. You'd better be careful, because I may have to tunnel right under you, and if I loosen the earth around your legs, you may tumble over. Ho ho!"

The scarecrow listened – and a bright idea flashed into his turnip head. Of course! That was just what he wanted! If only he could get his wooden legs loosened from the earth, he would be free to walk!

"Mole, tunnel right under me!" he begged. "Do. Do!"

"You'll fall on your nose!" chuckled the velvet mole. "You will! How I shall laugh!"

"Yes, you do it and laugh!" begged the scarecrow. "It is sure to be funny. Go on, mole."

So the mole dived back again into the earth and began to tunnel at top speed towards the scarecrow, throwing up mounds of earth as he went. Very soon the scarecrow felt the mole at work round his wooden legs and he knew that the earth was becoming very loose there.

The sun sank down. Darkness came over the field. The birds went to roost in the trees and in the ivy. Still the mole worked around the scarecrow's legs, trying to make him fall down on his nose. And at last down he went, flop! His hat rolled off and a large piece of earth went into his right eye.

But did the scarecrow mind? Not a bit! He was as glad as could be.

"Ho ho ho!" laughed the mole, and went on his way to tell all his friends what a joke he had played on the scarecrow.

The scarecrow tried to pick himself up, but it was very difficult. He tried and he tried. The night grew darker and the scarecrow felt frightened. Suppose he couldn't get down to the rabbit-holes before the moon rose? It would be too late to warn everyone then, for the Princess would be taken prisoner before the moon came!

At last he managed to pick himself up! How strange he felt with his legs out of the ground! He picked up his hat and put it on.

And then he got a shock – for he saw creeping along by the hedge at the bottom of the field, the two witches! Yes, there was no mistaking their tall pointed hats.

"Too late, too late!" groaned the scarecrow in dismay. "Oh, dear, oh, dear! The rabbit-carriage will be by at any minute now!"

He tried to stagger along down the field and, dear me, once he got going, he couldn't stop! The field was steep and the slope took his legs along very fast indeed.

Suddenly he heard a scream, and he knew what had happened. The rabbit-carriage had come along with the Princess and her attendants, and the two witches had stopped it. Down the field staggered the poor old scarecrow, and as he went, he yelled at the top of his voice:

"Beware, you bad witches! Here comes the great wizard Boolamoolahippitty-twink with his scratching nails, his pointed teeth, and his terrible spells! Ooooooooh! Beware! I come, I come, the terrible wizard Boolamoolahippitty-twink!"

What made him call out all this he really didn't know, but he felt that he must try to frighten the two witches somehow. And he certainly did!

When they heard this strange song coming out of the darkness, and saw, with their green witches' eyes, the strange, stumbling figure of the scarecrow, with his bowler hat on all crooked, and his scarf flying out behind him, they felt quite sure it *was* a wizard. They had never heard of the wizard called Boolamoolahippitty-twink, and no wonder, for there was no such person but they quite thought it must be some fearfully powerful magician, and they were frightened almost out of their lives.

They screamed loudly, jumped on the two broomsticks they had nearby, and sailed away into the sky at top speed. How glad the scarecrow was! He looked about for the Princess Peronel. There she was lying on the grass, looking as scared as could be.

"Princess," said the scarecrow, in his hoarse, woodeny voice, "Princess, I've come to . . ."

"Oooooh!" shrieked the poor Princess, in fright. "Go away, you horrid wizard! I'd rather have the two witches than you! Go away!"

"But I'm not *really* a wizard," said the scarecrow, humbly. "I'm only a scarecrow, and I must beg your pardon, Princess, for daring to come near you, ugly old creature that I am. But you see, I *had* to rescue you from those horrid witches. I couldn't get anyone else to help."

The Princess sat up and looked closely at the scarecrow. She saw his funny round turnip face, his stick of a nose, his wooden legs and arms, and his ragged old clothes – and she knew he wasn't a wizard, but only a poor old scarecrow. Very soon he had told her everything, and she listened in silence.

"You must forgive me for frightening you like this," said the scarecrow. "I know I am not fit to come near such a beautiful creature as yourself, Princess – but, you see, there was nothing else I could do, was there?"

The Princess went up to the scarecrow. She put her warm little hand through his wooden arm and squeezed it hard.

"I think you're a darling!" she said. "You are a dear, brave, clever old scarecrow, and I want you to come to Pixieland with me and be my scarecrow! I grow fine peas there all the year round and the birds do steal them so. But if you are there, the peas will be safe. Will you come?"

Would he come! The scarecrow couldn't believe his ears! He couldn't believe his eyes! To think that this should have happened to him, an ugly old scarecrow! Well, well, wonders never cease.

He found his voice at last.

"I'd love to come, Princess," he said. "But I can't. No, I can't, it's no use."

"But why not?" asked the Princess in surprise.

"Because I'm too dirty," said the scarecrow, mournfully. "Much too dirty, and too ragged. I'd be ashamed to come to Pixieland like this."

"Oh, is that all that is worrying you?" asked the Princess, with a laugh. "How silly of you!"

She touched him lightly with her wand – and a strange thing happened. The scarecrow's bowler hat turned to gold. His scarf became red silk. His coat was made of thick brown satin with a thread of gold running through it, and his trousers turned to bright silver. My, he looked a real prince!

His turnip face was bright with joy as he saw all these wonderful things. The Princess touched him again.

"This is to make you able to walk and run like ordinary people," she said. At once the scarecrow found himself able to walk to and fro without staggering and stumbling. He was full of delight.

"Oh, Princess!" he said, kneeling down before her, his wooden legs bending quite easily beneath him. "You are too kind. Yes, I will come to be the scarecrow in your pea-patch. I shall be proud and honoured to scare away the birds for you. I shall walk all over your pea-patch and shout and wave my arms. Not a single pea of yours shall be eaten!"

"Well, that's settled, then," said the Princess, pleased. "Now, scarecrow, you shall come straight to Pixieland with me now. Look, there are my two fairy attendants with my rabbit carriage. Go and bring them here, and you shall drive me home."

Very proudly, full of joy, the scarecrow drove the Princess and her two attendants home to the palace. Everyone thought that he must be at least a Prince, so magnificent did he look in his grand clothes. It was only when they saw his turnip head and wooden legs and arms that they saw he was really a scarecrow.

Now he lives in the garden of the Princess Peronel, King of the pea-patch. The birds are frightened of him and never eat a single pea, which pleases Peronel very much. You should see the scarecrow walking up and down, waving his arms and shouting at the birds! He is so proud and so happy – but he did deserve his good luck, didn't he?

ENID BLYTON (1897-1968) IS PICTURED HERE IN 1951,
IN FRONT OF A BOOKCASE THAT CONTAINED
ALL THE BOOKS SHE HAD WRITTEN AT THAT TIME.
UP TO 300 MORE WERE ADDED BEFORE SHE DIED.

Other Books by Enid Blyton

On the next few pages is a small selection of Enid Blyton's books, arranged in order of publication. Many of them are the first in a series of books about the same characters; further titles in the series are given below each entry. The second publisher and date given indicate an edition that is currently in print and available in bookshops.

Adventures of the Wishing Chair

Newnes 1937; Mammoth 1992

A magic chair takes Peter, Mollie and Chinky the pixie on strange adventures during which they meet giants, goblins, witches and other unusual creatures.

Further titles in this series: *The Wishing Chair Again.*

The Enchanted Wood

Newnes 1939; Mammoth 1992

Beth, Frannie and Joe move to a cottage in the country and discover the Faraway Tree in a nearby wood. They make friends with the woodland folk and are taken up the tree to visit a succession of wonderful lands.

This is the Enid Blyton book many adults remember most clearly from childhood.

Further titles in this series: *The Magic Faraway Tree, The Folk of the Faraway Tree.*

Naughty Amelia Jane

Newnes 1939; Mammoth 1992

Amelia Jane is a doll who almost always behaves badly. The other nursery toys frequently get their revenge and Amelia Jane promises to turn over a new leaf, but her good intentions tend to be very temporary.

Further titles in this series: *Amelia Jane Again, More about Amelia Jane.*

Five O'Clock Tales

Methuen 1941; Mammoth 1993

This is one of Enid Blyton's many story collections for younger children.

The Twins at St Clare's

Methuen 1941; Mammoth 2000

Patricia and Isabel O'Sullivan have been head girls at their first school and are full of their own importance when they arrive at St Clare's as first formers. Now they have to adapt to being amongst the youngest girls. They only once make use of the fact that they are identical twins, but have fun, make good friends and learn how to get on with other people.

Further titles in this series: *The O'Sullivan Twins, Summer Term at St Clare's, The Second Form at St Clare's, Claudine at St Clare's, Fifth Formers at St Clare's*; two further titles (written by Pamela Cox) have now been added to the series – *Third Form at St Clare's and Sixth Form at St Clare's.*

The Mystery of the Burnt Cottage
Methuen 1943; Mammoth 1995

This is the first mystery for the Find-Outers, Bets, Pip, Larry, Daisy and

ENID, AGED 26

Fatty. Peterswood, the village where the children live, seems to be based on the village of Bourne End in Buckinghamshire, and is one of the few places used by Enid Blyton that can be positively identified.

Further titles in this series: *The Mystery of the Disappearing Cat, The Mystery of the Secret Room, The Mystery of the Spiteful Letters, The Mystery of the Missing Necklace, The Mystery of the Hidden House, The Mystery of the Pantomime Cat, The Mystery of the Invisible Thief, The Mystery of the Vanished Prince, The Mystery of the Strange Bundle, The Mystery of Holly Lane, The Mystery of Tally-Ho Cottage, The Mystery of the Missing Man, The Mystery of the Strange Message, The Mystery of Banshee Towers.*

The Caravan Family

Lutterworth 1945; Mammoth 1997

The first book about Mike, Belinda and Ann who live in all sorts of different homes and go on various types of holiday.

Further titles in this series: *The Saucy Jane Family, The Pole Star Family, The Seaside Family, The Buttercup Farm Family, The Queen Elizabeth Family.*

First Term at Malory Towers

Methuen 1946; Mammoth 2000

Darrell Rivers arrives at Malory Towers, keen and enthusiastic but aware that school life is likely to be very different from how it is described in school stories. She makes good friends, works hard and has fun.

Further titles in this series: *The Second Form at Malory Towers, Third Year at Malory Towers, Upper Fourth at Malory Towers, In the Fifth at Malory Towers, Last Term at Malory Towers.*

ENID, AGED 20.

ENID WITH HER TWO DAUGHTERS
IN 1946.